STAR TREK
THE NEXT GENERATION®

DO COMETS DREAM?

S. P. SOMTOW

**Based upon Star Trek: The Next Generation®
created by Gene Roddenberry**

POCKET BOOKS
New York   London   Toronto   Sydney   Singapore

An *Original* Publication of POCKET BOOKS

POCKET BOOKS, a division of Simon & Schuster, Inc.
1230 Avenue of the Americas, New York, NY 10020

This book is published by Pocket Books, a division of Simon & Schuster, Inc., under exclusive license from Paramount Pictures.

ISBN: 0-7434-1130-7

First Pocket Books printing July 2003

10 9 8 7 6 5 4 3 2 1

POCKET and colophon are registered trademarks of Simon & Schuster, Inc.

Manufactured in the United States of America

For information regarding special discounts for bulk purchases, please contact Simon & Schuster Special Sales at 1-800-456-6798 or business@simonandschuster.com

"INITIATE THE SEQUENCE," RIKER SAID.

"Sequence reinitiated," La Forge said. "Five minutes."

The computer resumed the countdown. *Four minutes, fifty seconds—forty—thirty— Three minutes, ten seconds—*

"No!" Troi screamed suddenly. "No, no, no!"

She had reacted before even realizing what she was reacting to—a harrowing pang of loss and disillusion—a cry of pain that had lasted for millennia could not be heard because there was no organ of speech to cry out—the desolate, stifled wailing of a lost child.

"Is something wrong, Counselor?" Picard asked.

"Trust me on this, Captain! Stop the sequence!"

Picard nodded. Riker held up his hand. *Sequence on hold at two minutes, twenty-seven seconds,* said the computer.

"Something is alive on that comet!"

*this novel is dedicated to
the members of the Bangkok Opera Chorus,
who didn't realize I was in the back of the hall,
typing away at this book, when I should have been
paying attention to them. . . .*

Contents

Part One:
The Reluctant Ambassador

O bringer of death
I love thee,
O lord of destruction,
I praise thee,
In thee alone
The circle closes
The end begins
The beginning ends.
Fire-breather, dark embracer,
Silence my heart
As it cries out in transcendent joy;
Still my last leap,
Snuff me out
At the climax of love,
For thou alone
Art my secret self,
And the shadow of my secret self,
And the love that is death.

—From the Book of Final Songs
            in the Holy Panvivlion

Your Excellencies:
The advisory board on preliminary consideration of worlds for Federation status wishes to place the following document into the record. It's been arriving in fragments; a quark star's gravity field seems to be disrupting the subspace communication system. Nevertheless, we do feel that it provides valuable secondary insight into the Federation's investigation. For your information, Dr. Halliday has been living quietly on Thanet for the last two years, gathering a not inconsiderable mass of information about their culture.

We're going to leave you alone with the Halliday report, Jean-Luc. Take your time over it. But not too much time, of course. We want you to decide what is right for yourself, and for the Enterprise, *of course; but it also needs to be right for the Federation. There are issues that you need to wrestle with.*

After the big conference with the senators and representatives, after the formal dinner, the dress uniforms, the delegates, the delicacies from remote star systems, it still boiled down to one man, one decision, and deniability.

Captain Picard had encountered so many new civilizations in his career. But he knew there was no magic formula for dealing with them. Each one was a microuniverse unto itself.

Halliday's report, they told him, *is sporadic, sometimes barely coherent. The man's a genius, but he's also insane.*

I know the type, Picard thought, as he politely sipped the lightly fermented *peftifesht* wine, a Thanetian delicacy that Starfleet's replicators had only just figured out how to create—tactfully substituting placebo ingredients, of course, for some of its more hazardous intoxicants.

Picard had dealt with eccentric field xenologists before, but the report of Robert Halliday, former professor of xenolinguistics at Cambridge University as well as erstwhile researcher into obscure Vulcan rituals (for which he had been expelled from Vulcan for carrying his research a little past the point of propriety)—suffice it to say that Halliday's history was colorful.

They had left him in a womblike cubicle to examine the documents. A young ensign informed him that more would be forthcoming as soon as the computer managed to transcribe their curious format—good old-fashioned handwriting.

Even the fact that the report was actually written on paper, using what Commander Data might have referred to as a human-operated analog inkjet device—a pen—was proof of the man's eccentricities. But Captain Picard knew all about technophobes—he had, after all, grown up with one. It was just another detail to be filed away, added to the equation.

Calmly, he continued reading.

CONFIDENTIAL REPORT:

Dr. Robert Halliday's field notes

The Transcript continues:

—have been hard at work translating the Panvivlion, the Thanetian Sacred Text, into some of the languages of the Federation. Oddly enough, it works very well in Klingon; much of the same rigid codification of honor and caste.

Came across a curious myth in the Seventh Book, which is called *Holokinesthanasionosis,* which loosely translated means "the death and rebirth of the entire universe." I don't have it all done, but we might as well begin with this— *Thanopstru,* or "death-dealing star." It's rather

interesting how many of the oldest root words
in the main language here seem reminiscent of
the Greek and Sanskrit lexicon; but to speculate
on that would be at best a digression; you must
forgive the xenophilologist in me, sometimes
the very sound of an alien word sets me
off . . . but I was speaking of the myth.

*Five thousand years ago and a day, quoth the
sage Outrenjai, came a great thanopstru to the
world, and the thanopstru is the eye of the
almighty, and the hand of he-who-shapeth. And
the thanopstru descended upon the world, and
for a span of time did fire rain from the sky, to
cleanse the darkness from men's souls. And at
the end of that span of time, all knowledge
passed from the minds of those men who
survived the holocaust, and they became as
madmen, drinking blood and eating the brains
of the dead. The wisdom that had accumulated
over the last five thousand years was wiped
clean, and now resideth within the treasure-
chests of the dailong, who lie in the heart of the
deep.*

*And he that had once been highest became
lowest; and the power to rule passed into the
hands of the one child who had shown no fear.*

*And that child spake, and said: We shall
unlearn all that has been learned. For this is a
new heaven and a new earth, and the laws of
the universe are new laws.*

*For all old knowledge is as useless tinsel;
and for this, the almighty hath made the human
race as a newborn babe, to begin the cycle
anew; and he hath provided the thanopstru, to
return once more when the cycle closes; for
threescore and ten is the time of a man; but the
time of an age of men is nine hundred and ten
times threescore and ten.*

*And the coming of the thanopstru shall be
signaled with visions and visitations. And sign
of the moment of the world's end shall be thus:
there shall sound from the place of the most
high a great death-knell, which is called the
Bell of Shivan-SarŽ.*

*Do not resist the thanopstru, but greet his
coming with gladness and laughter; for death is
not death, but the doorway to a new existence;
everything that has ever happened will happen
again, and everything that happeneth now is
but an echo of an ancient happening; for all
time is but a movement inside a stillness; as the
hands of a clock seem to race against time, yet
circumscribe a closed and unchanging circle,
so creation itself; rejoice that you are born to
die, rejoice in your place in the cosmos, rejoice
in the dance of creation and destruction,
rejoice, for time hath swallowed its own tail,
and hath given birth to itself.*

—the interesting thing about all this—well,
it's not much different from several human

9

cosmologies, such as the cyclic view of history of the ancient Hindus.

—that's all fine and dandy, there's a hundred fatalistic cycle-of-history cultures in every quadrant. And yet there's something a little disquieting about this particular myth.

You see—and this *may* be a coincidence, for in a galaxy like ours with a trillion worlds, a trillion rolls of the dice, coincidences this monumental could occur—I've found evidence of a big natural disaster five thousand years ago. And then again, their entire civilization seems to have sprung full-grown out of nowhere . . . like the goddess Athena from the head of Zeus—if you know your terrestrial mythology, which, somehow, I doubt.

Oh, yes, Dr. Halliday, mad as a hatter—I know what you people say. Let me continue.

It's a two-pronged coincidence. Just as they discover (or, as their own mythology would say, rediscover) warp drive, just as they're ready to join (or rejoin) the community of worlds, the five-thousand-year cycle rolls around. People start to go wild. They believe in the end of the world—they believe so thoroughly that computers on this world are programmed to reset their calendars to zero at the cycle's end, there's no way of even expressing in their language very easily the idea of a straight timeline—so this end-of-the-

world fever sets in, a cross between fatalism
and "what-the-hell"-ism.

So what do you know? The prophecies are
right. There's a comet headed right toward
Thanet, and nobody's planning to beam out.

My suggestion is that the Federation do
something.

"Well," Picard said, at the breakfast conference
the next morning, "I think that Dr. Halliday's hit the
nail on the head. The Federation should do something. You have decided to send me, that's clear
enough. You've also decided to leave my instructions
very vague, because our actions may chip away at
that which we all hold most sacred—the Prime Directive. To save their civilization is to destroy it."

The round table had its share of ambassadors, ad-
mirals, and planetary governors. For half an hour,
they had exchanged pleasantries; but there was an
underlying tension.

Picard's words were met with silence, with indeci-
sion.

"I suppose the operative word here is *deniability*,"
Picard said softly.

And there was more silence.

It's lonely to be a starship captain. That went
without saying, was pretty much a cliché in the
world of Starfleet. Space had its share of lonely moments: the endless starstreams, the dislocation of
warping space-time, the silence between the stars;

but here, on terra firma, with the Golden Gate rising from the mist through the great bay windows of this conference room, it was possible to feel even lonelier.

At length, Picard said softly, "I will do what has to be done."

Chapter One

Artas

LONELINESS.

For five thousand years he had floated, balanced on the boundary of the real and the dream. *Who am I?* There were times when the question made no sense to him at all; and then there were those other times, when images came, pictures of a paradise so achingly real that he knew they must have been true once.

A meadow of gray-green grass. A breeze. A deep blue sky. A dark, mysterious sea. Clouds, too, silver clouds fringed with gilt and purple; the moon that danced and the moon that wept. A twisted tower wrapped in vines that writhed as they sucked the vapor from the rock.

Warmth. A warm body pressed against his. A warm feeling, racing through blood and tendon and tissue. A warm star bathing him in comforting radiance.

Where did these sensations come from? In the here and now, there was no warmth. The place he was in was cold. He knew it must be cold, even though he had no neurons with which to sense the cold; he had no bones to ache, no blood to freeze. But he still knew it must be cold, just as his barely conscious self was fueled by a memory of warmth, and he knew the absence of warmth to be called cold. He also knew he was not meant to remember this much.

Forget! Forget!

A stern voice. It reverberated within what must be his mind. He knew that the voice was there to be obeyed, that he had been created and programmed solely to show obedience to that voice, and that terrible things would happen if he listened to the other voices, the voices of warmth and comfort. He no longer remembered what those terrible things would be. Surely there was no worse punishment than this—eternal exile from the warmth.

Forget these images! Concentrate on what you are now! What are you? Say it! the voice intoned.

I am vengeance, he answered, *I am death.*

Death, said the stern cold voice. *And what do you bring?*

I am the bringer of darkness. For five thousand years that conversation had played itself over and over in the sterile wasteland that was now his mind.

And what else do you bring?

Destruction.
And what else?
Death.
But what was death? Was this not death already, this endless journey through eternal cold, this sterile emptiness?
And how shall death come?
By fire.
But oh, he thought, how long until that fire? How long until that cataclysm shatters the frozen night? He longed for fire. Even though it might last only a minute before the end came, at least that fire would not be cold.
The fire will come soon enough, said the voice, *at the end of the endless journey.*
Once, he thought, I ran in the hills. The light of two suns—a river of quicksilver—the dark eyes of a soft-spoken woman, and—
I had a name once!
No more.
I think I can remember it—I think I can—
Forget! Forget!
No! If I could only find the name—if only I could find the key to who I am again—and who these voices are—and—
Why? It will only give you pain.
But even pain would be better than—*nothing!*
Forget, child. Forget.
He traveled on, dreaming of warmth. The warmth had a name, if only he could remember it—he him-

self had a name, if only he could dredge it out of the darkness within.

Forget, said the voice.

I'm trying, he answered, *believe me. Trying to forget.*

Chapter Two

Engvig

ACTING ENSIGN TORMOD ENGVIG could barely contain himself. To be on the *U.S.S. Enterprise*—to walk the corridors of the most celebrated starship in history—it was almost beyond belief for a young man who had spent his entire formative years in a small town in Norway most well known for its Viking Village Theme Park.

Until his prize-winning essay, and the tantalizing possibility of a coveted scholarship to the Academy, the only ships he'd ever been on were the longships they used in the Viking raid reenactment, attended by tourists from all over the Federation. This was hardly the same thing at all. Everywhere he went, there were these living legends just standing around; that very morning, no less a figure than Commander

Data had told him to straighten his uniform! He didn't really know his way around that well yet, but that afternoon he managed to find himself in a bar.

It was jammed with people. There was so much to stare at; Tormod wanted to disappear into a corner and just observe. The heart-stopping panorama of deep space, the stars far thicker and more brilliant than the clearest night sky over the fjord—the unfamiliar accents of Ferengi and Klingon—the heady scents of alien concoctions hanging in the air— plenty of sensory overload for a country boy who once thought he'd have to live and die in Rissa.

This had to be the Ten-Forward lounge, celebrated in song and story—it had even made its way into *The Second Volsunga Saga,* a controversial epic poem in Old Norse that continued the adventures of ancient heroes into modern times. *I'll just stay nice and invisible,* Tormod thought, *and try to do the osmosis thing.*

There was a slight feeling of disorientation; he blinked; the panoramic vista was suddenly quite different now; where there had been stars there were delicate skeins of streaking light. But no one seemed to notice—they all just went on drinking and chatting. The miracle of warp drive, and to these people it was as humdrum as a change in the wind at sea.

"Well!" It was a woman's voice, rich and comforting. "I'm glad *someone* hasn't lost his sense of wonder."

"You read my mind!" he blurted out. Then he turned to see yet another Starfleet celebrity, Deanna

Troi, leaning against the wall and smiling at him. "Oh . . . excuse me. Of *course* you read my mind. You're—ah—I used to read about you."

He searched for words, was once again—as often in the past two days—at a loss. How could he tell her how he pored over every encyclopedia, every simulation, even old-fashioned printed books, for every detail he could glean about this ship, its crew, its fabled missions?

"I don't read minds per se," said the counselor. "But I do sense—your wonder. It's a beautiful thing. Why, you're blushing, Ensign. Have you met the captain?"

Only then did Tormod notice that she was standing next to his childhood idol, the man whose exploits he had followed in the news and in all those romantic space travel memoirs and adventure simulations as a boy. "Oh, my God," he managed to stammer, "I used to have a holographic collector card of you."

"Ah yes." Captain Picard winced slightly. "The Heroes of the Federation series. I don't know why they let them talk me into being on one of those."

Mortified, Tormod realized he had forgotten to call the captain "sir."

"It's all right," said the counselor, once again uncannily plucking the very thoughts from his mind, "I'm sure the captain will overlook it, just this once." And she winked at him. *Winked* at him! Almost as if he were one of them!

"Engvig, isn't it?" said Captain Picard. "They're sending them to me rather young, aren't they?"

"Well, sir, I—well, I wrote this essay, you see, and I won a prize that includes becoming an acting ensign and writing up a—"

"Yes, I know, I read your essay. Congratulations on your temporary commission, young man; I assume this assignment will give you the self-confidence you will need when you begin your studies at the Academy in earnest."

Once more, Tormod was taken aback. He could only stammer out, "Sir."

"Shall we give the young man a bit of a thrill?" the captain went on. "I know you probably believe we're going to be running around saving the universe every five minutes, but our presence in the Klastravo system is going to be merely ceremonial, I'm afraid. Still, why don't you wait on the Thanetian ambassador at the dinner in his honor this evening? He's got a child your age; perhaps you could practice diplomacy of a more informal sort. Help conduct a short tour, that sort of thing."

Tormod could hardly believe his ears. "But sir, I barely know the *Enterprise* myself yet."

"Then it will be a great journey of discovery for the two of you. You'll report to Mr. Tarses at nineteen hundred hours; he'll brief you."

"But sir—"

"Filing a protest, Ensign?"

"Well, sir, no, sir, I mean—I haven't had a very sophisticated life. I wouldn't know what to say. I mean, I never even went to a big city until I won that prize."

"Engvig," said the captain in all seriousness, *"never* let anyone look down on you for growing up in the country."

Then there was a twinkle in his eye and Tormod suddenly felt that this man, who had crossed the galaxy from end to end, who had fought battles, saved worlds, and held the fate of thousands in his hands, understood him, really understood him. That, he realized, must be how he inspired so much loyalty. After only a few minutes, Tormod felt ready to give up everything to serve such a man on such a starship. It would be worth it. What a gift this man had.

He tried to imagine what it would be like belonging to this crew for real, rather than just serving on a single ceremonial mission as a result of winning an essay prize. *I wouldn't just be standing around gaping,* he thought. *I'd volunteer something. Give of myself.*

"I could teach him how to sail a Viking longship, sir," Engvig found himself offering. "You can count on me."

"Make it so, Ensign. Now, I'm going to assign you to Mr. Tarses. He'll do what he can with you in the short time you have. Your things are on board already, correct?"

"Aye, sir."

"You will move your belongings to Mr. Tarses's quarters for the duration of this voyage. Live with him, eat with him, learn from him."

"Mr. Tarses—? Wasn't he the—"

Tormod tried to remember what little he could

about this character. Tarses—*Simon* Tarses, he suddenly remembered—wasn't exactly a collectible card from the Great Starship Captains series. The name had to do with something darker. Betrayal. Espionage.

"Wasn't he the what, Ensign?"

"I'm not sure, sir. But I think he was accused of—"

"Spying," came a voice. "Accused and aquitted."

The man who had entered the Ten-Forward lounge was not at all as Tomod Engvig imagined. He remembered the story now; before coming on this voyage, he had done copious research, and a picture of Simon Tarses had appeared as a footnote to an encyclopedia entry on *Espionage, Romulan*. That picture had shown a young, smiling face; this face, though still young in years, had worry lines. The episode had left its mark on him, still haunted him, perhaps. Tormod was suddenly afraid. He turned to Captain Picard, hoping for some reassurance.

But the captain was already off, making his way through the crowd, deep in conversation with Troi.

"Come on, kid," said Tarses. "Let's get you started around here."

"Yes, sir," said Tormod.

"Don't look so starstruck," Tarses said.

But, having heard Captain Picard's signature three-word command actually addressed to him in person was pretty overwhelming for the young ensign. *I'd better get over all this fast,* he thought to himself. *But I can't totally believe that the* Enterprise*'s presence in Klastravo is "purely ceremonial." Everything I've heard and read about this ship points in a different direction.* Nothing *about the* Enterprise *is ever routine. It might start off routine, but it never ends up that way.*

And though the captain had just cautioned him about his youthful fantasies of saving the universe, he wasn't ready to let go of them just yet.

Chapter Three

Simon Tarses

THE LAST THING Simon Tarses wanted was a little camp follower. The acting ensign's simple adoration of everything about Starfleet, including this half-Romulan with a shadowy past, however, made it impossible to dislike him. In fact, the kid kind of grew on him after a while. He was a short pale fellow who nevertheless saw himself as a seven-foot-tall Viking, and that in itself was rather sweet.

Now, having been assigned the slightly delicate mission of steering Ambassador Straun's child around the ship, which showed a much-needed level of trust from Captain Picard, he was also being saddled with baby-sitting this essay-contest winner from some village on Earth. Still, some trust was better than none at all.

After all, it hadn't been that long ago that he had been the poster child for every Romulophobe in Starfleet's upper echelons. Now that the fuss had died down, there had occasionally been some reverse discrimination instead—those who claimed that his Romulan ancestry had triggered a "guilt reflex" to get him attached to the better, less routine missions.

As they left Ten-Forward, Simon regretted being so curt with the acting ensign. "I didn't want to say it in front of the captain," he said, "but you may save the universe yet. On the *Enterprise*, nothing is ever what you expect."

"I gathered that," Engvig said, "from my studies. In fact—now that I think of it—I *have* heard of you before."

"I was once the subject of an impassioned speech," Simon said, "about liberty, and truth, and the core values of the Federation." He tried to make it flippant, but even the kid could probably tell that Simon's wounds had not yet healed.

"I didn't mean to—"

"It's all right," Simon said. "Just don't take those core values for granted. *Never.* Promise me that."

"Yes, sir." He snapped to attention. Somehow, it made it seem like an act of devotion, of faith. He sure had a lot of innocence in him; Simon hoped it wouldn't crash and burn. As it had with him.

As they wandered farther down the corridor, Simon felt strangely protective of the young man. He wondered whether Picard had felt the same way about him. After all, there had never been any need for the grand starship captain to defend one minor officer.

"What do think he's like?" Engvig said. "I mean, this—ambassador's child we're supposed to look after?"

"Diplomatic brats come in all shapes and sizes," Simon said, "but they're usually trouble. Not in themselves—it's not their fault their parents are who they are—but because diplomats are all too human."

"Even aliens?"

"Just an expression," Simon said. Engvig blushed.

"There'll be a short quiz next period," he said.

"Yes, sir," Engvig said.

"I was just joking."

"I haven't totally learned when people around here are joking or not, sir," said Engvig.

"How old did you say you were?"

"Seventeen, sir."

"I see. No wonder. Well, people will be pulling your leg a lot around here. Goes with the age."

"Yes, sir. But—what were you saying about diplomats? It was very interesting."

"Like everyone else they love their children. And that means that when galactic politics are at stake, a little trouble their children get into can accidentally change history."

"Sir, we're walking right past Ambassador Straun's apartments."

The kid had the *Enterprise*'s geography memorized. "Don't show off," said Simon.

"I won't, sir," Engvig said, chastened.

The two stopped in front of the guest quarters and Simon announced himself. And suddenly, the child of Ambassador Straun sar-Bensu stood before them.

More than a child. A young woman.

"I am Kio sar-Bensu," she said. Her eyes were downcast.

They did not speak for a moment. When Kio looked up at last, she shaded her eyes with hands that opened to reveal a dainty vestigial webbing that had been darkened with a purple cosmetic dye.

"My name is Simon Tarses," Simon said. "I have been assigned to show you around the starship."

She didn't respond at first. And then Simon saw, in the background, her father, studying him with a stare that was both disdainful and a little fearful. She looked back at her father; he nodded.

"It is an honor to greet you in these end times," said Kio sar-Bensu softly. "May you return in a more elevated incarnation level than the lowly body you are about to leave behind."

Simon was taken aback, then remembered that these people were new to the idea that there existed anyone other than themselves in the universe. And they believed that all civilization was about to end in a matter of days. It was a ritual formula they used. But formula or not, the words had a special poignancy coming from her lips. Very soft, full lips—Simon shook himself. What was he thinking?! The very last thing he could afford was a romance that would undoubtedly spark an interplanetary incident. Captain Picard would be furious; worse yet he'd be disappointed. . . .

Ensign Envig was staring too, he then noticed with some chagrin. Another dangerous sign. Smart, enthusiastic, eager—and full of raging hormones!

He wondered whether he could find a tactful way to ditch the little guy, to spare his feelings if nothing else. After all, if Kio sar-Bensu was out of Simon's league, Envig didn't have a snowball's chance on Vulcan with her.

Tarses offered his arm to the diplomat's daughter.

Kio sar-Bensu stared at it for a moment, nonplussed. "To lead the way," he explained. "To steady you. So you can have someone to lean on in this unfamiliar wilderness."

"You are very charming, Mr. Tarses," Kio said sweetly, "and I'm not quite as alien as you think—though on our world, fraternizing between the castes would be considered, well, a little—gauche."

"We have no caste system on the *Enterprise*," Simon said.

"Exactly," said Kio sar-Bensu, smiling again, "and thus I forgive you, and take your arm with gratitude, in the spirit in which it is offered."

He led her down the corridor. The Norwegian followed at a distance.

"Have you ever been in a holodeck?" Simon asked.

"No," Kio said. "It sounds—exciting."

"Oh it is," said Simon. "It's a place where *anything* you can possibly imagine—can be real. And anything you *don't* want to imagine—can be made to disappear," he added, barely resisting the temptation to indicate the ensign with a flick of the head.

Chapter Four

Straun sar-Bensu

AMBASSADOR STRAUN SAR-BENSU felt like the pretender he was, after having been beamed aboard this impressive floating alien palace, greeted with astonishing pomp and cacophonous music, and now shown to quarters that would have impressed even the High Shivantak of his homeworld. He had, after all, arrived without any honor guard, without any of the usual bevies of pleasure maidens, attendants, dancers, and acrobats that would normally accompany even a minor envoy to a backwater tribe. He had come only with his child Kio, whom he had brought only because the young one surely needed a little diversion, a taste of what might have been, if the world were not coming to an end in seven more moon-turns.

That five thousand years of glorious history

should come to this! But that was the beauty of the eternal cycle, the grand encirclement of time, the perfect mandala of existence.

His whole life had been a journey toward the Pyrohelion, the grand extinguishing of all existence that had been prophesied since the beginning of history. It had been his highest honor to have been born in the last days of the world, to be privileged to witness the moment when one cycle would end and another begin.

The young, of course, did not truly understand.

Poor Kio. The child was occupied right now—they had sent some of their own young ones as entertainment, to show off the mysteries of this alien vessel. Why open his daughter's eyes to all this wonder, when soon those eyes would be closed forever? It was a paradox. Surely, in these end times, there should be a closing of doorways, a sense of resignation—not the sudden opening up of a million new possibilities.

And yet—

The coming of the *Enterprise* had not been prophesied.

Well, not strictly, not with quite the precision that so many other things had been.

What was that curious verse in the Panvivlion?

When the moment shall come and the world shall cease to be, there will come harbingers of false hopes, and the young shall dream of that which might have been; yet the thread of the times has already been spun, and the maker shall return to the unmaker, and the mandala shall be rendered perfect.

Was the *Enterprise* a harbinger of false hope? The High Shivantak had certainly thought so. But he had to deal with it.

Man shall not grow wings, nor shall he penetrate the veil of eternity.

Straun recited the familiar verses to himself, making the sign of the grand circle over his eyes with a thumb and forefinger. The ritual comforted him.

He remembered his audience with the Shivantak.

—the aged one, seated on a throne of gilt and raven-lizard skin, his ceremonial crown of meter-tall chlorquetzal tailfeathers catching the light of the Moon That Sings, four celestial maidens prostrate at his feet—

"You are Straun sar-Bensu?" The voice was heavy with age and care. Straun remained with his face to the floor, not daring to gaze directly at the Shivantak's face.

"Yes, Your Radiance," he said humbly, "I am a third undersecretary in the department of labor allocation."

"You are now an ambassador."

"Your Radiance! Surely not I!"

"True, you have not the qualifications. Indeed, your file shows a certain—lack of piety at times, even a questioning of the Ultimate Truths within the Panvivlion. Normally you would be sent to a reeducation camp, but in these last days, much is not as it should be. We require someone with a slightly . . . skewed vision of the world. There is a false prophet."

"Your Radiance?"

The scent of copal-frankincense wafted through the throne room. In the distance, a woman intoned the evening call to prayer.

"Men have grown wings in the last few years. But you knew that."

"Yes, Your Radiance. Your priests of science have visited some nearby stars in the new lightrider ships. And you have encountered aliens that resemble us greatly."

"The only body part they lack is the vestigial webbing we have between our fingers and toes," agreed the Shivantak. "And it is that very similarity that makes their heresy all the more terrifying. They have planted doubt in the minds of some—" and at this moment, Straun chanced to look up for a moment, and he saw in the venerable leader's eyes a flicker that might suggest that even *he* doubted—He quickly looked down again. The thought he had just had was unthinkable. The entire cosmos would collapse if the hierarchy of belief and truth were shattered.

"Do not be surprised that you see what you see," said the Shivantak. "I am not a god. These are strange times; that's why I haven't summoned one of the high priests, one of the star readers, or even one of the guardians of ancient wisdom, but a lowly third-class clerk. You see things I cannot see, with your viewpoint, close to the level of the common castes. There are those who say that the circle need not close itself; that the cosmos need not die and be born again in fire. Some of my most trusted priests, in fact, have come to read the Panvivlion differently from the orthodox view. And they've asked—these aliens, these creatures in their star-flying palaces—for help. Indeed, taking advantage of the confusion of these end times, they have convinced this—*Federation*—that the call for help comes from us—from the office of the Shivantak himself. And this *Federation,* this organization of worlds and creatures far vaster than anything our history has ever told us about, has responded. In friendship and in kindness. To avert the end of the world. They do not even imagine that the world is ending; they believe that to divert the Deathbringer is a simple thing, a matter of mere technology; they do not begin to understand the deep truths our history has taught us. You see, what I fear most is that they may even be right. And if our world does not end—then, in another sense, our world *will* end. Because truth itself will have crumbled to nothingness."

"Your Radiance," Straun said, "truly the things you speak of are beyond the imagination of a third undersecretary such as myself. Yet I am pledged to serve you; my life and my devotion are yours, utterly and irrevocably."

"Do you see even a glimmer of my great plan?"

"Not really, Your Radiance."

"I will fight deception with deception. As they come with a false hope, so shall I send a false ambassador. I meet falsehood with falsehood. I shall not deceive you, however, Straun sar-Bensu; you are in danger."

"And yet, Your Radiance, if the world is indeed ending in a few short moon-turns, that danger is meaningless."

"I know. And that is why I trust you. You may draw from the treasury what you need to make a show of it; let's not have these galactic travelers think we are so utterly provincial."

And the Shivantak had dismissed him with a wave, and turned to the ministrations of his pleasure women. In the end, Straun had not drawn massive amounts from the Shivantak's bursary; what was the point? He wasn't to be a real ambassador, but a pawn in the Shivantak's battle against heresy—a battle that was being waged even now, mere days before the end of the world.

He had collected his child from the seminary, paid a swift visit to his dead ancestors' ashes, laid in the Mnemo-Thanasium next to the Temple of Karturias; and then he had boarded one of the newfangled lightriders, with a crew of just three, for the rendezvous with this *Enterprise*.

Enterprise! The very name felt barbaric. A race that valued the concept of "enterprise" enough to name starships after it! How bizarre. They surely had no idea at all that every creature in the universe had its proper place in the grand mandala. It was probably every man for himself in their culture—

competition instead of cooperation, everyone ignoring their caste, even, Brahmat forbid, equality between sexes and races! Truly, the Shivantak had cast him into a den of ferocious Konaubeasts. And Kio's enthusiasm for the journey made things all the more awkward.

There's nothing I can do about all this, Straun decided. "There's nothing I can do about all this" was perhaps the most common saying among his people, who believed above all that everything in the universe was preordained, that everything had already happened and would happen again. Still, it was comforting to think it. Contradictory thoughts were dangerous, bewildering—even bordered on the heretical.

He adjusted his robes, shifted the links in his chain of office, repainted the webs between his fingers with the colors of authority, and applied more silver dust to his wig, repeating three times the incantation to the Controllers of Fate, as he had done each morning before dusting the computers in the department of labor allocation.

And sat in meditation, awaiting what fate would bring next.

Chapter Five

The Labyrinth

SHE WAS EXTRAORDINARY. Simon had never encountered anything like her, her delicate hands framed by fragile webbing, her eyes of deepest mauve, their almond shape surmounted by angular eyebrows and a swirl of dark blue hair. Kio siv-Straun sar-Bensu wore a garment composed of a web of single-celled organisms, a living fabric that changed color according to her moods as it fed on the pheromones secreted on her skin. The garment was accentuated by what looked like a large insect, attached to her shoulder by a golden thread, its chitinous exoskeleton a spectrum of iridescent colors.

When he thought about it, he realized that Engvig's presence was more of a blessing than a burden. Though the acting ensign may not have seen himself as the perfect chaperone, he was unwittingly playing that role. For Kio, who was clearly warmer and more demonstrative than most people from her world, was oddly reserved when Engvig was around. Simon didn't know whether to feel relieved or disappointed, so he continually switched back and forth between the two reactions.

"Come," he said, "I'll show you what we do to amuse ourselves."

Someone had left an ancient Earth mythology program—*Theseus and the Minotaur*—running. It seemed a suitable choice, what could be dryer, less romantic, safer, than an old story? As they entered, corridors led in all directions. The fearsome howl of some kind of nightmare creature echoed, amplified by the cavernous walls, covered with murals of naked youths performing acrobatics with raging bulls. Simon didn't know the specifics of the tale, but he dimly recalled hearing it had something to do with a ball of yarn and a terrifying monster. So perhaps it was not quite as dry as he had thought, but it certainly didn't seem romantic, which was a good thing. Or so he tried to convince himself, as he saw Kio's exquisite deep-set eyes grow wide in wonder. "Somewhere in this so-called *labyrinth* there's a giant man-devouring bull, and we have to find it and exterminate it," he told Engvig.

"We'll have it mopped up in no time," the acting ensign said, "and the universe safe for humanity once more." And—plucking a great sword that seemed to materialize out of thin air—he ran down a corridor that, by the magic of computer morphing, twisted and corkscrewed into another and another out of sight, and was gone.

"I forgot to tell him about the ball of yarn," Simon said.

"Yarn?" Kio asked him.

"The hero ties it to the portal, thus—" The yarn popped into his hand, and Kio was suitably impressed, and he tied one end to a doorknob that had also just sprung into existence, in a spanking-fresh door that had just opened up into another sequence of corridors. "—and so Theseus is able to find his way back after killing the monster."

Kio gasped. In place of her somber "end of the world" garment, there was a diaphonous Greek chiton that seemed to have been spun from the sheerest thread—from cobwebs. From moonlight. Simon looked away, tried to concentrate on the murals, but the barely clothed frolicking youths pictured therein didn't distract him as he had hoped. They seemed to mock him instead. Why had Picard chosen him for this assignment? And where was Engvig! A breeze from the tunnels stirred Kio's sweet-smelling hair.

"Mr. Tarses—Simon I . . ."

"Shall we look for the monster?" he interrupted her. She looked irritated. Probably thought he was rude, which wasn't the worst thing that could happen under the circumstances. This was an odd sort of diplomacy, though, in which making a poor impression was preferable to making too good an impression. Simon tied the other end of the yarn to his belt and resisted the temptation to take Kio's hand as he led her down the hallway.

The floor of the corridor appeared unsteady. Then it became a sporadic vibration—an unnerving sound at the threshold of hearing—the footsteps of a great beast—"The minotaur!" Simon said.

"And you're going to fight it off? To protect me?" Kio beamed at him.

"Uh, actually it's getting a little late. Why don't we leave the monster to Mr. Engvig."

"And what will you and I do?" she said, placing her delicate, webbed fingers on his shoulder. Tarses swallowed.

Sheepishly, Simon said, "How about a tour of the ship?"

"Will you show me your quarters?" she asked quickly.

"Why don't we start with Engineering?" he countered.

He had been showing her the different levels of the ship, and she had been fascinated by everything, even by those details whose scientific explanations he himself was barely able to understand.

Luckily when they got to his quarters, Ensign Engvig was already back from the holdeck, setting up shop. Instead of the neat, spartan furnishings, there was a huge model of some kind of primitive sea vessel with a dragon's head and little round shields down the sides.

Simon turned to Engvig. "Back so soon?"

"Yes, sir!" said the young man. "Killing that monster was a snap. I suddenly remembered about it from Mythology 101, so I got myself a ball of yarn. I really appreciate the lesson in problem-solving, sir!"

"I have a problem you could solve," Kio said coyly.

"Yes, ma'am!"

"I'm getting awfully thirsty. Could you possibly fetch a drink for me from that lovely room with the starscape?"

"Ten-Forward? Certainly!"

And he was gone. Kio beamed at Simon. Simon called after Engvig, "Don't be long!"

"So barren," she said, "so sparse." It was true. Apart from Engvig's bags, of course, and that longship model. Now that the boy was gone, he found himself staring at it. It was rather fascinating, and he did remember, vaguely, stories about adventuresome Vikings in his studies of Earth history—a compulsory subject at the Academy, and one of the least relevant, some said.

"It looks just like a *dailong*," Kio said. "Do you think this Earth of yours once had them?"

"What's a *dailong?*"

She laughed. "You don't know? It's a sea dragon, so vast that you could build a city on its head. And we do."

"I doubt that Engvig's little ship is long enough for that," Simon said.

She was endlessly fascinated by replicators. Simon watched, amused, as she tried to figure out how many Thanetian native dishes had already been programmed into its repertoire. It seemed that almost every dish it produced was forbidden to her; these people had a complicated system of caste, and each caste was allowed only certain foods.

"Every caste eats in its specified restaurants," she said. "Don't you have that? It's the only way to stay pure. I'm not sure that replicator food would really qualify."

"On the other hand," Simon said, "it's not 'really' food made from 'real' ingredients."

"That's true. It's a fantasy." Boldly, she took a bite of the *xeriposa,* a kind of chocolate snail. She looked for a moment as if she was going to choke, but she kept it down—and then she smiled. "Wow. I haven't been struck dead by the Lance of the Eternal Tartillion."

Simon realized that she had made a major leap of faith. It might have seemed a small step to him, but she had crossed a bridge, transcended her pocket universe to touch the great galaxy beyond. Simon had had to make the same leap once. To leave his nebulous past hiding his Romulan heritage—to bind his identity, his future to that of the Federation. And with that leap of faith had come many bad things. Accusations and a traumantic witch-hunt. But wonderful things, too. Picard's impassioned defense of his rights. And his continuing association with this fine ship, this fine crew.

Even the awe in the shining eyes of that young acting ensign wasn't so bad, even if the kid did tend to disappear at the most awkward times. What was taking him so long anyway? Suddenly Tarses understood why Kio had chosen Ten-Forward as Engvig's destination. She knew. Just from looking at the kid, she knew he couldn't resist lingering, hoping to catch another *Enterprise* celebrity in a moment of relaxation so he could chat them up. Simon winced at the thought of his charge pestering Commander Riker, or worse yet, Worf.

"I could almost forget," she said, "that you people are all just shadows, specters of what-might-have-been, that you're just here to haunt the final days of the world—just as was foretold in the Panvivlion, the book all honest souls must live and die by." Her lilting voice broke his reverie.

He knew he should not contradict her. Civilizations in their myriad forms are sacrosanct—that was the philosophy behind the Prime Directive and the whole rationale of Starfleet's attitude toward other worlds. But he couldn't help himself. He didn't want her to believe that she was doomed. He knew she didn't want to believe it either.

"What if—what if—" he began.

"I know what you're going to say," she said. "The

Panvivlion warns us that in the end times we will be sorely tempted."

Tempted indeed, Simon thought. But it was not his place, he knew, to tempt this beautiful and perceptive young woman away from any of the beliefs or practices of her world.

"I'd better escort you back to your father," Simon stammered.

Chapter Six

The Banquet

THEY HAD SET UP the banquet hall in Holodeck Four instead of one of the great reception lounges. This was all about setting the Thanetians' minds at ease, surrounding them with the trappings of their own culture. It was particularly important to tread lightly, since the Federation had only become aware of the Klastravo system's civilization about a year before, and though the Thanetians had indeed achieved space travel, they did not seem to have the worldview of starfarers.

Dominating the dining hall was a fifteen-meter-long statue of a *dailong,* one of the giant sea serpents that seemed to be a very important part of Thanet's watery environment, and which seemed to figure in many aspects of their civilization.

Picard did not feel particularly comfortable in the

Thanetian ceremonial headdress with its bright purple and neon green feathers. Still, one had endured far worse in the pursuit of galactic friendship.

Right now Commander Data was preparing Captain Picard and the senior crew members for the various eating rituals. Bemused, the captain watched the android explain the entire thing in earnest, grave tones, though what they were actually about to do had a touch of the theater of the absurd about it.

"You will have to grasp the neck of the ravenlizard with your right hand, Captain," he said mildly, "like so." He held up the holographic animal, which seemed to have the temperament of an annoyed mink. "And then snap it with a deft flick of the wrist, allowing the juices to run into the left bowl of the double goblet. Then, raise the goblet with your left hand, twirl the stem so that the effervescent liquor from the right bowl begins to trickle through the filter."

"A people who kills what it eats at the dinner table understands the spirit of the warrior," said Worf with unmistakable admiration.

"We are not actually killing anything, Commander," Data explained patiently. "This is a holographic simulation. Only the ambassador's party will actually perform any animal executions. But, in the interests of diplomacy—"

"Diplomacy," the Klingon snorted. Picard fought the urge to smile. There were certain constants in the universe and Worf's cantankerousness was one of them.

"It is my understanding that the killing of the raven-lizard is supposed to represent the subservience of all life to the laws of the great mandala of existence."

"What *will* we actually be eating?" asked Dr. Crusher.

"I believe you will find that yours has been imbued with the texture and taste of something more familiar and pleasant to yourself."

She took a sip. "Chocolate pudding!" she exclaimed, as much in irony as delight.

"Computer," Data said, "give us the grand council chamber of the palace of the High Shivantak."

Around them, columns shot up in the air, each one carved with cunning images of gods and goddesses—many of the poses, to say the least, a little risqué. Murals painted themselves across stone walls, and again the scenes were of hunting, dancing, and amorous pleasures. A ceiling began to form above their heads, and there were more images of love and pleasure in all its forms.

"Those Thanetians sure know how to live!" Dr. Crusher said with a smile.

"Or how to party at any rate," said La Forge, whose ravenlizard had managed to escape unscathed, and was now running around on the banqueting table, uttering strange hooting noises.

"I fail to see how one can know how to live," Data said. "Living is not a learned phenomenon."

A silvery moonlight filtered in through gauzed bay windows; from the other end of the chamber came a ruddier light, a different moon, for Thanet's night sky was graced by a complex dance of satellites.

"Computer," Data said, "intensify the hue on that second moon. It is not quite as I recall." The room became moodier; vivid red light washed over the stone carvings.

When Picard looked more closely at what appeared at first to be images of hedonism, he saw that the culture was haunted by death as well as love; for intermingled with all those scenes of pleasure were little reminders of mortality. A bedpost topped by a human skull looking over intertwined lovers; a rotting corpse peering from behind a curtain.

No question about it, Thanet was an interesting place.

"They are on their way," Data said. "Shall I commence the welcoming music?"

Picard nodded. When the music began, he smiled. This, at least, was familiar: Kamin's classic arrangement of Mozart's clarinet concerto for Ressikan flute and bamboo organ—a piece the captain himself had played once, in a memory shared with that great ancient musician.

The music complemented the holodeck program perfectly, smoothing over what would otherwise have been a most garish spectacle. Lightveils parted to reveal the ambassador, who was garbed in several layers of robes and extravagant headgear. The webs between his fingers were painted, and there was a patterned circle intricately painted on his brow, a miniature mandala. The ambassador seemed agitated. "My child!" he said. "Kio has not returned to my quarters."

Commander Data asked the ship to locate Simon Tarses. No sooner had he spoken than the illusory veils of light flew open to reveal the young crewman and the ambassador's daughter. Ensign Engvig was skulking in the background.

"*This* is your guide? Captain Picard, I must protest. I assumed you would have picked someone more suitable, an older woman, perhaps, or—"

"Oh, Father, really," said Kio.

"I meant no harm, Your Excellency," said Tarses. "I was just showing her how things worked. And then, Ensign Engvig got lost—" Tarses glared at the poor boy who hovered anxiously in the background.

"I had trouble getting back to Mr. Tarses's quarters from Ten-Forward."

The ambassador raised an eyebrow.

"Oh, Father, nothing happened!" She appealed to the captain. "On Thanet, they think they only have a week left to live, so people have been wildly giving way to, well, their baser instincts. These people aren't like that at all, Father," she added. "Their planet isn't about to be crushed to smithereens. And if it were, they'd *do* something about it."

"Heresy!" the ambassador exclaimed. But she only laughed.

She was as captivating as her father was ungainly,

in a simple flowing garment of *sarducca,* a living, sheer fabric woven from one-celled creatures that grew into angstrom-thin filaments and lived off the fluids secreted by the human organism.

Captain Picard frowned. He had hoped for a less negative reaction from the ambassador, but was not particularly surprised that the selection of Tarses had not gone over well. Truth be told, Picard himself would have made a less controversial choice, if Crewman Tarses had not been the next name on the roster for guide duty. But skipping over the young officer would have sent the wrong message to Thanetians, to Starfleet and to Tarses himself; a message that a half-Romulan could never be trusted, even with the simplest assignments.

"Your daughter, Ambassador, is perfectly safe with Mr. Tarses, as she is with any member of my crew," Picard said in a voice that he hoped broadcast his intention to brook no further insults to Simon Tarses.

Straun opened his mouth, clearly wanting to reply, but then apparently changed his mind. He glared briefly at poor Tarses, who looked utterly miserable, and then stomped off the transporter pad, causing the colorful metallic ornaments on his hat to knock into each other and rattle in an echo of the ambassador's indignation. It was time to break the tension.

Picard smiled, signaling for the Mozart-Kamin to begin once more. "I trust you find this venue a little more familiar than the alien corridors of our ship. Shall we sit?"

Soon the officers and diplomats were all seated, and ravenlizards' necks were being snapped, both holographically and in the flesh; Tarses, the captain noted, did well after a moment or two of hesitation, while Engvig seemed to have no trouble serving the various beverages.

The first half of the dinner was taken up with pleasantries. How lovely your world is, congratulations on having recently conquered space, and most of all, How impressive the *dailong* look as they breach and sound from Thanet's tempestuous oceans.

"Yes, it's a stirring sight, Captain," the ambassador, seated on the captain's right, was saying. "It's so sad that it must all end soon."

Silence fell. It was time for the real business of the evening.

Picard glanced across to Counselor Troi, seated at his left. She gripped the double goblet hard; no doubt she was experiencing Straun's feelings of hopelessness and fear.

"Must," said Picard, "is a difficult word—when one is speaking of the destruction of an entire civilization."

"Yet it is something we have been taught all our lives to expect, Captain," said the ambassador. "It is no great burden to know that our existence is circumscribed, that the circle must one day close upon itself, that we are both the end and the beginning of things."

"Even when that end is so easily averted?"

"Averted?" The ambassador seemed appalled. "It is indeed an honor, a miracle, that the gods have afforded us this glimpse of the greater universe at the moment of our destruction. But no, of course we do not seek aversion. That would be heresy!"

"Heresy?" said Picard.

"The High Shivantak would never permit such an outrage."

"And yet, Your Excellency," said Commander Data, "we have the High Shivantak's letter."

A holographic scroll appeared in the air above the dining table. It bore the great seal of the Shivantak himself.

We thank you for your enlightening us, the document began, *about the nature of things beyond. If what you say is true, let it be tried. Let us at least have a chance for life.*

The ambassador gazed at the document—and seemed ever more confused and mortified as he skimmed the words. "This *must* be a forgery," he whispered. "You are trying to subvert all we believe in."

"I fear that it is not," Picard said.

The ambassador's consternation was genuine, Picard realized, not some diplomatic feint. There was more going on here than met the eye. Perhaps this was not going to be a quick errand of friendship after all.

Ambassador Straun continued to stare at the hologram. *Deception!* he thought. Now who was deceiving whom? Was it these aliens, and did they have some strange agenda of galactic domination? No scripture mentioned what might happen if the world were *not* to be destroyed every five thousand years. The Thanetians would surely have no moral right to exist—perhaps they could even be reduced to a zombie-like state of slavery.

An even more frightening possibility was that it was the Shivantak himself who—

No! The holiest of the holy, profaning the very beliefs he existed to protect—beyond belief! And yet—

Nothing, thought Ambassador Straun, *is certain anymore.*

In a subdued voice, he said, "I will listen."

Picard said, "Mr. Data will explain the situation, and Mr. La Forge will show you how we propose to solve it for you."

Straun listened.

"Your Excellency," Data said, "there is a belief on your planet that all civilization comes to an end every five thousand years with the coming of a fiery star, a harbinger of destruction whom you call Deathbringer. The belief is so deeply ingrained as to have the force of fact. And there are other facts that seem to lend support to your cyclical view of history. For example, your recorded history is only five thousand years old, and there is definite archaeological evidence of a huge cataclysm at the very beginning of your history."

"Of course it has the force of fact!" Straun exclaimed. "Why would it not?"

"Please hear me out, Your Excellency," said Data. "I have analyzed all the information available to me so far, and the descriptions of the Deathbringer in your scriptures and in your literature and art are about ninety-seven point two percent consistent with the hypothesis that this instrument of destruction is in fact some kind of comet. Comets, as you know, are satellites with a highly eccentric orbit that brings them very close to the sun, then carries them far off beyond the boundaries of the star system. A five-thousand-year orbital cycle is not uncommon. Perhaps, the cataclysm of five thousand years ago was a near-collision of some kind during the comet's last cycle. If so, it would explain the belief in a five-thousand-year cosmic cycle, and also why civilization seemed to start up so quickly and so abruptly from what seems to be almost nothing."

Straun sat in stunned silence, but he could see that Kio was listening, not in shock, but in awe and—hope. He wanted to stalk out of the room at once, to call out the full forces of the antiheresy league with its inquisitions, dogma trials, and executions of false prophets, but the hope in his daughter's eyes was something he could not turn his back on.

The future is the past, said the opening lines of the Panvivlion.

If she really believed in a future, the ambassador thought, could he dare to take it away from her?

For her sake, he continued to listen.

Now it was the dark-skinned one's turn to speak.

This man, an engineer or scientist, it seemed, wore a strange prosthesis about his eyes, as did the Priestesses of the Oracle when they breathed the sacred fumes of Ar-Jan-Fang in order to interpret the commands of the gods. Perhaps it too had some kind of oracular function. Certainly it lent him an aura of religious mystery, and when he spoke his words were full of multisyllabic conundrums such as the priestesses were wont to insert into their utterances in order to render perfectly simple prophecies more dramatic-sounding.

"We have confirmed," he said, "that there is indeed a cometoid object on a trajectory that would intersect the inner Klastravo system within a few hours. We can anticipate actual collision with Thanet in about seventy-seven point three standard hours."

"So our scriptures are correct," said Straun, as relieved by the confirmation of his beliefs as he was mournful about the death of Kio's dreams of a bright future.

"Yes," said La Forge. "But the collision won't happen, sir. The prevention of comet disaster is pretty routine; we can fine-tune our phasers to pulverize it long before it reaches Thanet's orbit." As he spoke, the hologram of the Shivantak's missive vanished and was replaced by a schematic of the Klastravo system. They had plotted the Deathbringer's path; a fiery comet was winging its way toward their planet, the whole represented in miniature with such lifelike accuracy he could almost reach out and cup the entire world in his hand.

There it was. The end, as foretold, as sung about in a thousand odes. The Deathbringer inexorable, implacable. But then, from the edge of the viewing area, a starship materialized. The *Enterprise.* A few quick bursts of light, surgical in their accuracy, and the Deathbringer was no more. Just like that.

"Would you like to see that again?" La Forge said.

Ambassador Straun nodded numbly. Seeing was believing, but the third and fourth replay were not enough for him. His master—the High Shivantak— already knew of this. He had sent him—an under-secretary, a *nobody*—into this place. Straun was being set up for a heresy trial—he was sure of it! But what difference could all of this plotting make so near to the end of the world? Unless the Shivantak did not plan for the world to end! Unless the un-thinkable were true—and in his heart of hearts, he knew it must be. The Shivantak was a consummate politician. If there was a way he could cling to power, to life, and an undersecretary could be sacri-ficed, a heretic who had somehow manipulated the aliens into saving the world—a heretic who could be made a scapegoat—it made a twisted sort of sense. Set up to take the fall!

Or am I just paranoid? he wondered.

"Forgive me," he temporized. "It is all so over-whelming."

"Perhaps—something familiar will ease your mind," Picard said. He clapped his hands; the holo-gram of the Klastravo system dissipated. In its place was a platter of poached cassowary eggs topped with whispering algae from the snowy slopes of Iliman-tang. The kind of delicate dessert that graced only the tables of High Shivantaks and their priestesses of nocturnal pleasure.

"Not that familiar," he said wryly. He had always wanted to try Cassowary eggs. If he still believed that his life, that his very world, was coming to an end, he probably would have reached for one. But now his arm felt numb and his stomach roiled. The past hour's events had caused the ambassador to lose his appetite for even the most intriguing confections.

Reflexively he glanced at his daughter, hoping to find comfort in her beautiful face, but her eyes were fixed upon that boy—that *crewman. Wonderful,* he thought sourly. *She's falling in love with a barbarian, and a low-status one at that.* Couldn't she at least have picked a high-ranking officer. Now she would not just die in shame. She would live her last moments in shame. Just wonderful.

Picard's voice intruded on his thoughts.

"We have the Federation's formal response to the Shivantak's letter," said Picard, and two crew members in dress uniform entered the holographic chamber bearing a gilded chest on a silver tray covered with feathers. They bowed in keeping with Thanetian custom, and handed the tray to the ambassador, who waved his hand over it three times and inclined his left wrist in the formal gesture of acknowledgment.

He then waved it away, and the two crew members retreated with it to the background.

"I shall carry the message to my master," he said.

But who was his master now? Was the Shivantak now a heretic himself—and thus no longer worthy of allegiance? Ambassador Straun kept these mysteries in his heart, and bowed humbly even as he cursed these aliens for trampling on everything he had ever believed in.

Chapter Seven

Artas

AND STILL HE FLOATED.

Subtly, imperceptibly, the dreams were changing. The voices were strident, urgent. He wanted to wake up. He hadn't felt that way before, not since the journey began.

He dreamed of lights. Twinkling red lights. More voices. Alarms. Levers. Switches. Twisted ribbons of metal glistened in the half-dark. This was very different from the fields, the ocean. Usually his dreams were nothing but warmth, nothing but softness. His dreams were there to help him forget the cold hard metal prison that was his whole existence . . . but now, something impinged upon that inner paradise. Something was changing. The journey was truly ending.

This was strange.

There was something out of place.

Forget! the voices screamed. He was afraid.

Or—another memory surfaced. Tantalizing.

Are you my mother? he asked the alien voice.

It did not answer him for a long time—but finally, with a certain sadness he did not think he had ever heard before, the voice said, *No.*

If only I could weep, he thought to himself.

He could not quite remember what weeping was, but he knew he would feel better afterward, because someone would enfold him in her arms, and he would sleep.

Chapter Eight

Asylum

SOON THE TRAUMA would be over. Ambassador Straun was relieved to be returning to Thanet, even though he knew that he would soon be facing a confrontation with the High Shivantak.

A heresy trial, perhaps? In a way it didn't much matter. Infamy or honor, all would be washed away when the great cycle returned to its beginning, when the mighty Ur-Dailong swallowed its own tail, when the karmic quotient of every soul would have its counter reset to zero. Unless . . . No. He must banish all doubt. These were the teachings of the Panvivlion; these were the sayings by which he lived.

At 0900 hours by the aliens' curiously rigid system of reckoning time, he was walking toward the transporter room with this disturbing bald man

whom they called "captain." The hospitality he had
received aboard this vessel would of course be recip-
rocated on Thanet; a lavish reception was planned,
and a party from the *Enterprise* would attend. Some
were there already; there was that obscene parody of
a human being, the android who spoke in riddles,
and a few others he dimly recalled from last night's
dinner. This creature seemed to be exhibiting a
bizarre hyperactivity, breathing heavily, with his
hands trembling and his lips constantly trying out
different smiles and frowns.

At length the ambassador couldn't control his curiosity and said, "Are you ill, Mr. Data? You appear
abnormally agitated."

"I am attempting to demonstrate the proper level
of excitement," said the android. "I am about to set
foot on a world new to the Federation. It is an excep-
tionally thrilling moment, hence I am causing my
extremities to palpitate and increasing the pace of
my heartbeat and breathing. It is all part of learning
to fit in with humans, Mr. Ambassador."

"In our culture," said the ambassador, "we place
great importance on *never* trying to become what
one is not."

"You *are* overdoing it a little, Commander," said
the captain mildly.

The commander immediately went very still. It
was unnerving, how the creature could switch parts
of itself on and off. These were an unholy race indeed, for they blurred the distinctions between the

highborn and the lowborn . . . even between the animate and the inanimate! He would have a great deal to report to the Shivantak, assuming that they didn't hustle him off to a heresy trial within minutes of his return to the real world.

His daughter was due to meet them there. In a moment of weakness, he had permitted her out of his sight, for a last-minute tour of some sort of menagerie. She loved animals. He loved her, wanted above all to humor her wishes now that their time together was so limited; he hated the handsome young man they had assigned to escort her everywhere, distrusted the way he tried to anticipate her every whim. But it was only for an hour. Then it would all be over. Yes. So it was written. He would believe.

He and the captain reached the little chamber with the instant-travel machines. She was not there.

"Ah, young people," said Captain Picard. "They do love to keep us waiting."

Straun didn't like the intimacy that "us" implied, so he just smiled grimly. "My patience is not infinite," he said.

Several long moments passed.

The captain continued to smile. Oh, those reassuring glances, those ever so patronizing looks! This alien actually *pitied* him. He thought he was some deluded, self-destructive fool, and not the guardian of his world's eternal truth.

"What have you done with my daughter?" Straun said, succumbing to a sudden panic.

"I'm sure she is on her way," said Captain Picard, his voice oozing the serenity of one who does not have his own daughter to protect. Truly, these people were insufferable!

"Computer—location of Kio and Crewman Tarses," the Captain continued seemingly into the empty air.

"In Holodeck Two, Captain," said a disembodied voice.

"Beam them here immediately," said Picard to the transporter technician.

A flash of rainbow light, and there they were. In mid-embrace. The temerity of it! Straun was trembling with as much agitation as the artificial human had shown earlier in his obcene mockery of human emotion.

"Father, I can explain—" she began. Meanwhile the young man was hastily concocting lies to soothe his captain—some nonsense about the constant presence of someone named "Engvig," and the trio's innocent stroll through something called "the buffalo exhibit." Quite suddenly, the boy claimed, Straun's daughter—his decent honorable Kio—had thrown her arms around Tarses's neck. To even suggest such a disgrace—it was simply unbearable.

"I was just—entertaining her. Obeying orders," the boy concluded lamely.

Kio was not at all sheepish after she recovered from her momentary embarrassment. "Entertaining me! Is that what you call it? You've shown me doorways into other universes, you've tugged at my heartstrings and my emotions, you even caused me to break the sacred laws of the Panvivlion and—you call it entertainment? Were you entertaining me or myself? Were you just toying with me?"

Simon Tarses just stood there, his lying mouth hanging open, his eyes stupid with shock. Picard frowned, but held his tongue.

A monumental rage stirred in Straun. A day and a night among aliens—and his daughter had practically become one! What had they been doing in that so-called holodeck, what filthy alien secrets had she been learning? And what if she had somehow already yielded up—her precious *ara-ta-zorn,* that thing which may never be yielded to a man without the seal of approval of the Shivantak's Conjugal Affairs Office? It was all too much! In his life, he had never so much as said a harsh word to his daughter—he had left all the disciplining to his late wife—but this was the last straw. He was going mad. He threw aside all diplomatic pretense and pulled her to him. His bony hands went for her throat.

"You bring shame on me, you—you—*arataq!*" he screamed. There! The most insulting word in the Thanetian language had escaped his lips.

Kio twisted free. And then—and this was far worse than if she had wept, or spat back some insult—she began to laugh.

"Is this what it's come to, Father? Your world is about to be pulverized by a comet, and you still want me to protect my purity? For what?"

S. P. Somtow

"Captain!" Tarses protested. Picard's palm covered his brow as he shook his head in dismay.

"Not my world, daugher—*the* world. Our universe. The very hub of our existences."

"Father," she said, "I've tasted sweet *zul* from the mountaintops of Aragur! I've sipped the juices of the forbidden purple pomelo! Those are the highest taboos in our society, Father! After that, what's a little sex?"

Ambassador Straun slapped his daughter's face. Immediately, he felt a strong hand grip his arm, presumably to restrain him from striking her again. He looked up into the angry eyes of Jean-Luc Picard.

"That is enough!" the captain thundered. But the human needn't worry. Straun would not raise his hand to his sweet, innocent daughter again. None of this was her doing. These words weren't her words. Henceforth he would lay the blame where it belonged. Right at the feet of Simon Tarses.

"I swear, sir, I never, never in a thousand years. . . ."

"That's enough out of you too, crewman."

"Father," Kio said, "I'm not going back." To the captain, imploringly, she turned and said, "They can't make me. I'm going to *die* if I go back. Everyone's going to die, and they don't even care."

"No one's going to die," said the captain. "I've given the Shivantak the Federation's word that this disaster will be averted—"

"How dare you!" Straun cried. "Isn't it enough that you've shamed me in front of my daughter by forcing me to stoop to—violence? Isn't it enough

66

that you've sown the seeds of doubt in her, so that she can no longer face the end gracefully, with quiet stoicism and pride?"

"Captain," said the young girl, "I demand—I don't know, political asylum!"

"I didn't mean to—I was telling her about some of Earth's ancient history—the Cold War, people defecting, that kind of thing," said the young man forlornly. "I didn't realize that—"

"Mr. Tarses, we will discuss this later in my ready room. Dismissed." The young upstart left. Straun silently promised himself that he too would have words with Tarses. Later.

Captain Picard put his hand on the girl's shoulder. She continued to stare defiantly at her father, but Ambassador Straun was not inclined to back down.

Gently, the captain said, "Kio, your father is an ambassador, and we are in the process of establishing diplomatic relations with your world; perhaps now isn't quite the time to—"

"A world that is about to be destroyed. You're never going to succeed in blowing up the comet," said the girl. "My father is a fanatic. He'll sabotage your plan. He'll subvert even the High Shivantak himself—"

"Heresy!" shouted the ambassador with all his might.

"Heresy, he says," said his daughter. "Well, then . . . if not political asylum . . . I claim religious persecution. I don't believe in the inevitability of the end of the world . . . and my father is trying to force me to die for my beliefs."

"Kio," Picard said softly, "you must go with your father. I cannot interfere with the traditions of your people."

"Cannot?" she said, as slowly she moved toward Straun, looking away when he tried to embrace her. "You already have. I wish, oh, by the Panvivlion, I wish you had never come."

For the first time that day, Ambassador Straun agreed with his daughter. Change had come at the eleventh hour, bourne by this mighty ship.

Change!

Nothing had ever changed on Thanet.

The universe is a dance. The cycles follow each other with the regularity of—no! Nothing *has ever changed on Thanet,* Straun found himself saying over and over in his mind, as though the repetition of that axiom were enough to counter the clear evidence that change had finally come.

And Straun was afraid.

Part Two:

The Machine That Was Mortal

Do not resist
The one who shall come
For the one who shall come
Is father and mother to you
And son and daughter as well;
You are all part of the chain of being
As the dailong, engendered deep beneath the sea,
Rises from the mists to serve you
And retreats beneath the waves
When his time is come;
You are all as the dailong,
Called by God,
Sent back by God
At the proper time.

—From the Seventh Book of the Holy Panvivlion

CAPTAIN PICARD, once more, was alone with the report. Halliday had the unerring knack of putting his finger on that which was most troubling to the Federation, that which the Federation most wanted to avoid coming to grips with.

For the Prime Directive, beautiful as it was, was an idea, not a law of nature.

It had taken millennia for this idea to be shaped, and yet it was still as fragile now as it had been when first formulated. So many things worked against it: avarice, human desire, megalomania, even love.

Picard read on:

CONFIDENTIAL REPORT:

Dr. Robert Halliday's field notes

Dr. Halliday's report resumes with more translations from the Panvivlion, and his commentary:

As far as I've been able to figure out, the Thanetians have seventeen basic castes, each of which is divided into hundreds of subcastes, and the amazing thing is they keep it all straight. Every caste has its own ritual greetings, its own respect language, and its own dietary restrictions. The dietary restrictions, in particular, are spelled out with astonishing strictness in the Book of the Forbidden, the lengthiest section of the Panvivlion. I have been working on one such segment, and this gives the general flavor:

"Of the flesh of the he-*klariot,* no part shall be partaken of that lieth betwixt the organs of digestion and the organs of breath; for such tissues are the exclusive right of the priestly clans. But of the she-*klariot,* such flesh may be freely eaten, provided that four ceremonial sips of *peftifesht* wine are taken between each bite, and that the she-*klariot* hath not been known to have had carnal congress with any male of a species other than its own."

The *klariot* is small mammal, about the size of a Denebian possum. By the way, its flesh is very delicate, and it's not perhaps that surprising to an aesthete such as myself that the various bits would be so jealously argued over in a religious text; imagine, if you will, a really fine filet mignon with a hint of caviar and a sort of musky aftertaste.

The truth of the matter is that it is so hard to ascertain the correctness of the diet, and the stigma attached to making a mistake is so severe, that there have developed special restaurants and grocery depots for each caste, and even the large hypermarket chains that cater to all have separate exits and entrances for the seventeen major groups. It would seem to me that replicator technology would make a lot of sense in this culture, since the entire Book of the Forbidden could be programmed into it. However, there is a section of the Book of the Forbidden that implies that the use of replicators might not be religiously acceptable.

The Thanetians attach great importance to their laws, their hierarchy; ceremonial forms of address are used even in the home, among close relatives; and the first question asked of a stranger is often "Where do you sit?" a way of finding out what level to assign to the person and what forms of address to use. Indeed, a formal living room is designed more like a very wide staircase than the flat floors we are used to; and those of higher caste automatically gravitate to the highest step.

I have tried to find out the origins of this tradition, and have been told only that it is lost in the mists of time.

However, we have already determined that "time" on Thanet only goes back five thousand years; those mists are more in the nature of an iron curtain, completely separating this present civilization from its past.

I do not feel that such a sophisticated hierarchy could just have sprung from nowhere; I welcome the arrival of Federation savants who would help in gathering material. I particularly welcome the suggestion that Commander Data might join my efforts for a while. For while his physical form is human enough that the natives would not fear to give him information, his powers of deductive reasoning would undoubtedly be more than human. . . .

"Computer," Picard sighed, "inform Dr. Halliday on Thanet that an away team will be there very shortly. Including, as he requested, Commander Data."

Chapter Nine

Thanet

ADAM HALLIDAY WAS ONE of the only humans on Thanet, and certainly the only human child. That should have made him very precious, but in practice it made him a loner. His father was often so wrapped up in his research that they barely spoke for days at a time; sometimes Adam wished he hadn't come along, that he had stayed at the institute with the other kids. At least there would have been people his own age. Well, sort of. They weren't kids exactly at the institute. They had special talents, which made them bad company.

Adam too had a special talent. More than one. For one thing, he had a Betazoid great-grandmother, which, he was often told, accounted for his occasional flash of intuition. For another, he was a genius.

The best thing about Thanet was the fact that Adam was special. He wasn't a member of any caste—his off-world status made him acceptable everywhere. He could literally go anywhere in the city, walk into any shop, speak to anyone at all. And everyone wanted to be nice to him, pet him, stare at his unwebbed hands, run their fingers through his reddish hair.

Being special was the worst thing about Thanet too. He wished he could have a friend. Perhaps, today, he finally would; the Federation was sending down a team to look over his father's research.

They were arriving right now. They had just beamed into the courtyard. It was night, but the Moon That Sings flooded the stone walls, making the silvery flecks—a mica-like mineral—sparkle. They materialized next to a small shrine of Yarut, the love god, the epaulets glistening on their uniforms. Adam hid behind the well as his father emerged from the dilapidated hostel the Federation had acquired as its research headquarters.

Dr. Robert Halliday waddled out and greeted the guests with a wave. "Welcome, welcome," he said, "it's not often we get visitors here at the End of the World."

"But Dr. Halliday," said the one with the strangely rubbery skin and funny eyes, "this is not the End of the World at all; indeed, the *Enterprise* has come here to prevent that very thing."

"Irony, Mr. Data," said Adam's dad, "a little gallows humor."

"I see, Dr. Halliday," said the man.

Adam couldn't help giggling a little. This man was very literal-minded. Halliday shuffled over to the well and pulled out the boy. "My son," he said. "I asked him to help greet the new guests, but he prefers to play the spy."

"Ah, the famous Adam Halliday," said the man his father had called Mr. Data.

"I'm famous?" said Adam.

"It is rumored," said Data, "that an eight-year-old boy by that name at the Metadevelopmental Institute once scribbled out an astonishing proof of Fermat's Theorem on a piece of rice paper. . . ."

"And," his dad added, "in fit of pique at being denied his favorite pudding, swallowed the paper! Oh yes, that's my son all right. A genius manqué, but a genius nonetheless."

"Well, since you know so much," Adam sniffed, "I've figured out who you are, too—you're that famous android. And you're even smarter than me."

"That is very perceptive of you, Adam Halliday," said Commander Data, taking the backhanded compliment in his stride. "Allow me to introduce the rest of this away team. Lieutenant Lisa Martinez is a science officer on temporary assignment, an archaeologist and philologist—"

"I much enjoyed your treatise on the use of glottal stops in the regional dialects of the Klingon Empire," said Martinez, shaking Adam's father's hand.

Halliday made a dismissive gesture. "A trifle," he said. "But I've been working on something a lot more significant—I'm translating James Joyce's *Finnegans Wake* into Ferengi. Those people could use a little light entertainment."

"Well, son," said his father, "why don't you show the commander around the city later? Then Martinez and I can chatter through the night about obscure dialects. As for Mr. Tarses—you don't seem very happy."

"I believe he is suffering from what humans metaphorically call a 'broken heart,' " said Data, "although cardiac arrest does not appear to be imminent."

"Nothing that a good pizza can't cure, young man!" said Halliday. "Shall we dine?"

The child, Data thought, was a curious phenomenon. That evening, at dinner, he had not spoken at all; but the next morning, as he showed the commander through the crowded cobblestoned streets of the metropolis, he chattered so rapidly that even the android had trouble parsing the nuances of his speech patterns.

"See," Adam said, "up there, the endless zigzagging steps all the way up that artificial mountain— that's the High Citadel, and the High Shivantak lives inside it. He never goes out. He's like a kind of king, pope, and living Buddha all rolled into one. Did you enjoy the pizza last night? Dad sends in his food column, you know, the one under that pseudonym, he sends it in religiously to that magazine; he always has time to describe a meal, even when we're investigating the mating rituals of cannibals or something. Along those walls, those cloth drapes, they're the entries to the different food halls of the different castes, you see, they're all color-coded. Toss that beggar a coin. Don't worry, he's not as sick as he looks, they have a union and a special subcaste of their own."

A theater on wheels, pulled by two-headed quadrupeds, rolled slowly by, and on it two actors intoned and juggled simultaneously, while an eerie music blared from a quartet of instruments that looked like a cross between trumpets and cabbages. Children rushed after them, shouting epithets, singing along with the music. They paused for a moment when they saw the boy and the android, and then they started chanting, "Aliens, aliens," not viciously, but with a kind of lilting curiosity.

"Don't mind them," said Adam. "They come from the clan of theater children, and they spend their whole childhood learning to imitate others. Look." Adam held up his hands, wiggled his fingers, clapped, and scratched his head. The sequence was taken up by all the kids, and pretty soon there was almost a weird sort of ballet going. Adam stopped; they all stopped; and presently there were gales of giggling.

"Intriguing," Data said, uncertain of what he had witnessed.

They were descending now; the streets sloped downhill; indeed, everything in this city was full of slopes and stairs, for everyone had a need to be higher or lower than someone else; it was in their culture. For ease of movement, the streets had escalators, banks of them; those for the upper castes were inlaid with colored stones and cunningly wrought intaglios of the faces of gods and demons; the lower castes' escalators were plainer, and were crammed with people: merchants with cages full of squawking birds, pleasure women with their eyes heavily painted with gold dust, newsboys barking out the latest information from quaint little handheld monitors strapped to their arms. It was dawn, but several moons still danced among aurora-like veils of light.

"That play they're doing," Adam said, "it's a reenactment of the rebirth of the world. They have those all the time now, puppet shows, plays, cantatas, 'cause they all think the world's gonna end in like six or seven days, moon-turns they call them, and they're all kinda hysterical about it."

"I do sense a certain urgency to everything around me," said the commander.

"C'mon, Data, we gotta catch the ferry."

They had reached a canal lined with temples. A dozen harpists strummed at the water's edge. Adam translated their song:

*We greet the world's death
With great joy,
Laughing, we embrace
The beginning and the end;
Eagerly we wait.*

Halliday was already waiting for them with the rest of the away team. Small watercraft bobbed up and down as the canal broadened. Each craft contained a team of *dailong* hunters, young men in translucent wetsuits that gleamed, wearing elaborate headdresses that revealed their city of origin.

"Welcome, Data," said Halliday. "You're about to witness one of the more remarkable spectacles on Thanet—the hunt for the *dailong.*"

"The *dailong* are—a means of transportation, are they not?" Data inquired.

"More than that; they're an obsession, a planetary sport, and a cultural icon." Halliday beckoned to a passing skiff; it pulled alongside. "Hop in!" he said. Data and the boy climbed on. The boat was small, and powered, astonishingly, by oarsmen, who paddled with eerie precision as a drummer boy beat out a rhythm, singing:

*Oi-oi-o! Oi-oi-o!
We come,
Little and puny,
We come to capture
The great beast of the deep.
Oi-oi-o!*

The oarsmen pulled toward the lock, which clanged open; dozens of the skiffs plowed through into the harbor, and the chorus of oi-oi-o's resounded about them as the wind began whipping up the waves.

Simon Tarses was in his element—Mother had taken him sailing often when he was a child, which gave him something in common, thank goodness, with poor Envgvig. The briny smell of the moist wind, the bracing chill of the water as it splashed up with the oars' fall, the song of the drummer boys punctuated with raucous ululations . . . This world was so alive, so vivid—how could they all be so willing to renounce it all, to accept an ending?

He thought of Kio. He wondered where she was now, whether she was still thinking about him. He had tried, and failed, to stop thinking of her. If only she weren't so beautiful. The captain was right to reassign Tarses and his starstruck charge to the away team. One more day on the *Enterprise* and Engvig would have started asking the bridge crew for autographs. And Tarses would have been unable to resist kissing the ambassador's daughter.

The oarsmen rowed rapidly. The boats were sleek, brilliantly engineered; they sliced through the waves with eerie precision. These people were almost like Vikings—Ensign Engvig's ancestors, Simon thought. He remembered folktales about hunting the great whales amid the freezing northern waters, with only one's wits and the most primitive of weapons.

At the prow of each skiff sat a man or woman, each one cross-legged and apparently in deepest meditation. What were they doing? Each one wore flowing robes, and had an elaborate caste-mark on his forehead in the shape of a giant serpent—or perhaps a *dailong*. Some of them didn't look like they should even be on the water; some were frail and withered, some mere children. On the skiff they rode on, this figurehead sat on a carpet whose patterned fibers rustled and twisted as he mumbled strange incantations. It was an old man, a hundred years old at least, whose face was battered and pocked like the canyons of an airless moon. His white mane streamed in the wind.

"Oh, him," young Adam was explaining to Data, "he's the *dailongzhen,* the man who will ride the *dailong*. It's some kind of telepathy. Some people have it, some don't. I have a bit of it, well, more an intuition really, you know. And it's not really a Persian rug he's sitting on; it's kind of a half-sentient lichenlike thing that grows in the northern deserts; it acts as a telepathic amplifier."

"Couldn't have explained it better," his father said.

"Learned from the best," Adam said, grinning.

The oarsmen chanted. The boats, Simon realized, were in the shape of the *dailong* image he had seen in the ambassador's quarters on the *Enterprise.* Which meant they were very close to that model

Viking longship that was such an eyesore in Simon's quarters. Even the designs on the sails seemed the same, images of beasts and gods. About a hundred strong, the convoy moved in what seemed like anarchy at first; but Simon soon saw that there was an eerie pattern to the movements; the skiffs darted, listed, and wove in and out of each other in an elaborate choreography that only some god could see—or perhaps some monstrous sea creature.

Then came a cry—an elemental sound—thousands of oarsmen chanting in resonant unison as the waves crashed about them—*dai-LONG! dai-LONG!* All at once, the *dailongzhen*s of each skiff stood up, arms upraised, and punctuated the chanting with savage whoops and shrieks. All the boats turned at once, and what had seemed chaos now became precision as they fell into position and bore down on a position far out to sea, halfway to the horizon—

—and when Simon looked to where Adam pointed he could dimly make it out, a sinuous, serpentine shape that rippled about the waves, impossibly huge, breaching the bright water—metallic rainbow colors cascaded about it—a shimmering aurora hovered above the sea—

dai-LONG! dai-LONG!

—a monstrous finned tail now, lashing the waves, and—

They were moving unnaturally fast. Simon realized now that these were not the wooden oars of ancient times, but oars equipped with some kind of waldo that amplified the rowers' strength. The sails did not rely on the wind but on a man-made wind generator. Indeed, he saw now with wonder, the hull itself was not true wood, but a simulacrum, and the sail had a glow that unmistakably indicated a radiation-based source of power.

They were slicing through the water now, speeding toward an island in the mid-distance, an island that glittered in the searing blue-white light of Thanet's sun. Except that it was no island—no. The island was beginning to rear above the waters, and he could see eyes now, crimson, jewel-like. And in the distance, segments of the *dailong*'s serpentine body thrashed against the waters.

The island was the dragon's head, and before he could fully register that fact his boat, skimming the waves, was pulling up alongside, and the oarsmen, chanting to steady their rhythm, were pulling up their oars and hurling them at the creature's brow— the paddles were metamorphosing into harpoons with corkscrew points that whirred as they burrowed beneath the dragon's skin—Simon saw sparks fly from the scales—he gasped—was this some blood sport after all, like the whale-hunts of the ancient past—senseless and cruel? The chanting grew in intensity as the skiffs pulled up and each team cast their weapons. The dragon did not seem to resist. A bloodred rheum oozed from its eyes, each eye as large as a small shuttlecraft, the oily liquid spreading over the surface of the ocean.

"The *dailong* weeps!" one of the team members shouted. Presently the cry was taken up from all sides, over and over, a ritual mantra as the thick fluid seethed about the skiffs.

And all the *dailongzhen,* risen from their meditations, were now standing, making mysterious gestures at the dragon's head. "What are they doing?" Simon couldn't help asking.

Adam said, "They're trying to establish a mindlink with the creature. The first *dailongzhen* to break through will be the first to mount!"

As he spoke, the old man at the prow went into an ecstatic frenzy. A halo shone about his face as a string of nonsense syllables erupted from his lips.

"He's made contact!" Dr. Halliday said excitedly. "Data, Tarses, Martinez—this is quite the coup! Our team has won the right to enter the dragon's mind. I had hoped this would happen, but I never dreamed it. And on the evening of the world's destruction, too—what a thrill!"

"I thought the world wasn't going to be destroyed," said Simon.

"Maybe not," said Halliday, "but you'll never convince these people."

As the old man shouted his incantations, the oars that had become harpoons changed function yet again, growing metal tendrils which linked together, tightened, connected—building a causeway back to the skiff, a miniature suspension bridge.

"Very sophisticated," Data said. "It appears to be bioengineering of some sort—perhaps utilizing a rapidly reproducing species of titanium-fixing bacteria—"

But before they could say more, the *dailongzhen* was already walking across, one arm raised skyward. And the crew of the skiff were following him, chanting, "He has conquered the beast! He has tamed the creature of the deep!"

"If you start worrying about titanium-fixing bacteria," Dr. Halliday said, "you're going to miss the whole spectacle. I scraped a few samples on the last hunt; I've already mapped their genome; it's in the computer back at the mission. Don't underestimate these people, Commander—their social structure may be in Earth's Middle Ages, and their space travel may be antediluvian, but they do know how to splice a gene or two."

Data was about to answer when a trapdoor opened on top of the *dailong*'s head. Simon hurried to join the Thanetians who were scrambling toward the dragon.

"It's a machine," Lisa Martinez was saying in awe.

"Machine or animal," said Halliday. "The Thanetians aren't terribly particular. After all, they believe that the entire universe is a machine—a machine that cycles back to its starting point every five thousand years. They've got a sort of clockwork view of reality, don't you see."

Sentient or not, it was awe-inspiring. Almost enough to allow Simon to forget the expression on Kio sar-Bensu's face when she had been forced to return to her world.

Chapter Ten

The High Shivantak

"DO NOT SPEAK of him again!" Kio's father was berating her as the two of them waited in the antechamber of the High Shivantak's audience hall. They had been waiting for perhaps an entire moonturn—it certainly seemed that way.

"Father," Kio said, "he never touched me in an impure way. He's a Federation officer, Father—they have codes of honor, too, though *you* may consider them all to be barbarians. It was me, Father—I wanted him to!"

She had to admit that she rather enjoyed the look of horror in her father's face. She hadn't been able to get a rise out of him in years, and now, all at once, she was sending him into tizzy after tizzy. *Perhaps he does love me after all,* she thought.

"It's not enough that I've been made to lose my

way in the Shivantak's theological labyrinth like some laboratory rodent," he said, pacing back and forth, "not enough that I've been unable to enter a proper state of inner calm so that I can receive the world's ending with true joy in my heart—not enough that I've thought the unthinkable, I've actually suspected the infallible Shivantak of heresy— but my daughter has to choose this moment to rebel." So distraught was Straun that he actually collided with the wall, knocking a sconce askew, spilling liquid fire on the polished jasper floor. An attendant hastened to scrub it, muttering a mantra of omen-aversion as she wiped the tendrils of cool flame with a gilded sponge.

"Father, Father," she said softly.

A man had entered the antechamber. It was the High Shivantak's chamberlain. He wore a robe of black *anatir* feathers, and held the Orb of Judgment in his left hand. His countenance was grim.

"Lord Kaltenbis!" Straun said, kneeling as was appropriate before one whose brow bore the caste-mark of M'Thartush. "When will he see me? There is so much to report, so many questions that need answering, questions that could undermine the very fabric of—"

"Silence!" Kaltenbis shouted. The orb glowed. "His Radiance will not see you."

"He will not—"

"Not now, not, perhaps, ever, considering we are only a few moon-turns from the end of time. Yet, I am to tell you that he has considered your report fully. And further, I am to tell you that in my right hand"—he shook one flowing sleeve, and a sealed decree slid into his hand—"I bear your fate. This is—but you will already have grasped the implications from the glowing of my orb."

Kio gasped. Suddenly her father's discomfiture had assumed far more dire dimensions.

"Yes, it's an edict of execution with a finding of heresy. Shall I read it to you? I'll just go through the highlights: Straun sar-Bensu, being employed within the ecclesiastical demesne of the most high, etc. etc., stands condemned of contemplating the breaking of the great circle—"

"I?" said Kio's father. "I? I was the most loyal believer until—why, the High Shivantak himself—"

"Absurd," said the chamberlain. "You impute fallibility to the infallible—I should burn you at the stake with my own hands!"

Kio whispered urgently in her father's ear, "Father, now you see how treacherous they are. You *see* that they've used you to keep their noses clean while *you* take the fall for daring to find out for them the thing they most want to know—the thing it's forbidden for a citizen of Thanet to even think—they want to know if the Federation is telling the truth! Because, even if it destroys you and half the world—they want to cling to power! Half a world is better than none!"

She put her arms around her father's prostrate body. He was weeping now, his face racked with great sobs. Furious, Kio sprang to her feet. She looked the chamberlain right in the eye. "Look what you've done to him—look what you've done to this whole world—you are going to swallow the truth whole—and spit out a lie—you don't believe a word of the Panvivlion. Hypocrite!"

"Don't make things worse for us!" her father whispered hoarsely. "The shame of it—thank the great powers that the world will end anyway, and my being burned at the stake only shortens my life by a day or two."

"Arise, Straun sar-Bensu," said Lord Kaltenbis. "The decree of execution is but what I carry in one hand. But with the other I can give back what I shall have taken away."

He shook his other sleeve: another decree. Deftly, he switched the orb into his other hand. The second decree was not bordered with red, the sign of the purifying flames of execution; it had a green border. And the seal of the High Shivantak was on that one as well.

"In my other hand," said the chamberlain, "I have an alternate edict. The sentence of execution is hereby commuted until *after* the end of the world. Your honor is safe, as at that time you will have no goods to seize, no good name to besmirch. In return for these few days without shame, you shall continue to engage the Federation."

"Engage?" Straun said, his expression of terror and despair turning into one of bewilderment.

But Kio saw what the lord chamberlain meant

right away. There had been two possibilities: the great truth of the Panvivlion, and its opposite—the unthinkable. Between these two incompatibilities there must be a middle way. A loophole.

"You want my father to save you," she said slowly.

"We want him to continue to—examine the theological incongruities, to see if we can arrive at a more accurate interpretation of the Panvivlion," said Kaltenbis.

"And what could he gain from that?"

"He will gain—his life."

"I think my father will want more than his life. I think that he will want something higher—a change in caste."

"But caste is decreed by birth!"

"The High Shivantak," said Kio, "is the embodiment of the Panvivlion; the truth made flesh; he is infallible. Why can't he just command a change?"

"I shall raise the matter with the High Shivantak," said the lord chamberlain, and it dawned on Kio that a man so unaccustomed to questions easily crumbled in the face of a challenge. Even a challenge presented by an insignificant seventeen-year-old girl.

"Father," she whispered, gently pulling her father back to his feet, "we're going to have to revisit that Captain Picard again. And we're going to have to keep our minds wide open."

Chapter Eleven

The Comet

CALM RULED ON THE BRIDGE of the *Enterprise*. The officers at their stations, patiently monitoring the unfolding situation. La Forge was ready for the captain's signal to unleash, with surgical precision, the mighty power of photon torpedoes on the rogue comet. Counselor Troi watched; though this was a routine operation, she had had a strange foreboding about it.

On impulse power now, the ship moved with an eerie majesty through a gaseous mini-nebula that, though its matter was so thinly spread out that, bottled up on Earth, it would be considered a perfect vacuum, here shimmered with the borrowed reflection of a far-off star cluster. Thanet's sun, Klastravo, was veiled by the nebula, its light diffuse and mysterious.

"Another star system," Picard mused, "another civilization hurtling toward a doom perhaps created by its own folly—"

Truly, Troi thought, *the human condition is a universal constant—everywhere we go, we see the same glories, the same frailties.* She could sense the captain's frustration.

"The comet, Captain," said Commander Riker, glancing down at his array of computer information. "Closing in, trajectory as predicted."

"On screen," said the captain.

The image came into focus—a thing of lethal beauty. Its tail glowed against the starstream.

"Impressive," said Riker.

What a welter of emotions that one word held, Troi thought. The boyish enthusiasm for the exotic phenomena of space—that was still there inside the mind of the mature commander, coolly sizing up his opponent. A man versus a space-borne object the size of a hundred starships.

"And it will surely make for an impressive display," said Worf. "Can we blow it up now?"

Picard nodded to his second-in-command. "Commence destruction of the comet," Riker said, and La Forge initiated the sequence.

"Five minutes till impact," he said.

"Four minutes, fifty seconds," the computer continued the countdown.

"Wait, Commander!" La Forge said suddenly. "There's a signal coming in from—a Thanetian craft—asking permission to beam aboard—it's the Thanetian ambassador."

Riker said, "We do have plenty of time, Captain. The ambassador ought to be a witness to this; it's routine for us, major history for them."

"Agreed. Escort him to the bridge," Picard commanded.

He summoned Deanna Troi to his side. "Do you sense anything?" he asked softly as Ambassador Straun emerged from the elevator, flanked by ensigns. Behind him walked the daughter, whom everyone had last seen desperately pleading for asylum.

"Confusion—ambiguity," she said, sotto voce, reaching out, sensing the man's emotions whirling within the alien's mind. "He can't believe he's here. But—the daughter's mind-set is more interesting. She's almost a different person—reborn—in charge of herself and her surroundings."

"Greetings, Captain," said Ambassador Straun. "The High Shivantak sends me as a religious observer to your rites of exorcism. They may be futile against the Pyrohelion, which has been ordained since time began five thousand years ago, but he has asked that every moment of our history be officially recorded, even up to the final millisecond." He stopped to stare at the comet, which now filled the screen, almost eclipsing the fiery globe that was Klastravo.

"I'm sorry to speak out of turn, Captain Picard," said Kio sar-Bensu, "but there's an added bonus. If

the world should be destroyed, as the Panvivlion pre-
dicts, we would still be observing, and we would not
actually be *on* the world; there might be a loophole,
you see."

"Sacrilege!" Straun could barely get the word out,
but his daughter went on speaking.

"And in that case," she said, "I would humbly re-
submit my petition for asylum, this time as a sentient being without a homeworld."

"And I'm sure your petition would be approved,"
said Riker.

An ensign showed the visitors to some seats.
Again, Picard asked Commander Riker to start the
destruction.

"Initiate the sequence," Riker said.

"Sequence reinitiated," La Forge said. "Five minutes."

The computer resumed the countdown. *Four minutes, fifty seconds—forty—thirty—three minutes, ten
seconds—*

"No!" Troi shouted suddenly.

She had reacted before even realizing what she
was reacting to—a harrowing pang of loss and disillusion—a cry of pain that had lasted for millennia
and could not be heard because there was no organ
of speech to cry out—the desolate, stifled wailing of
a lost child.

"What is it, Counselor?" Picard asked.

"Trust me on this, Captain! Stop the sequence!"

Picard nodded. Riker held up his hand. *Sequence*

on hold at two minutes, twenty-seven seconds, said the computer.

"Something is alive on that comet!" said Troi. "It's so—intense, so—" A wave of nausea now. She almost buckled from the impact of it.

Riker was speaking now. "Captain," he said, "imaging suggests some kind of hollow chamber inside the comet—in the shape of a perfect octohedron."

"An artificial comet, then," said Picard.

"With some kind of intelligence, perhaps," La Forge said.

"More than intelligence—it has emotion," Troi gasped. "Raw, unfiltered emotion that's built up over thousands of years—"

"The Panvivlion was right!" cried Ambassador Straun, coming to life suddenly. "This is no natural phenomenon that a few concentrated bursts of light can dissipate. This is the hand of the gods! Of course it has intelligence—of course it has emotion—this so-called comet is the God of the Last Days, the Inconsolable, the Eater of the World, he that is called *Sorex Pyrohilael,* he whose name can only be uttered by—"

"Nonsense, Father," said the daughter, "I'm sure they'll find an explanation for it all in due course."

"Due course! They only have two days."

"A lot can happen in two days," Deanna found herself saying. "Miracles have happened in a lot less."

"Miracle or not," the captain said, "the presence of a life-form changes the equation entirely."

Then he turned to Troi, who was still reeling from the onslaught of emotions from the heart of the comet. "Do you think—"

"I know what you're going to ask, Captain," Troi said. "You want me to go in closer."

"You're the only one who—can feel with it."

"Of course. I'll do it."

"I want the transporter room on standby to beam you back the instant you reach a threshold you cannot safely tolerate," Picard said. "And—Riker will be with you."

On screen, against the sea of stars, the comet continued to streak toward Thanet, and Klastravo burned bright, a beacon of death.

Chapter Twelve

Artas

THEN, IN THE FINAL HOURS, he thought he could hear another voice.

Not the harsh metal voice that denied him his childhood; this seemed softer, this seemed, in the end, soothing. A flash: dark hair, ringlets, deep haunting eyes. But it was not his mother either. It was a stranger. She knew neither his name nor even his species.

She spoke to him across the gulf of space. And time as well perhaps, though time had little meaning to him anymore.

She said to him, *I'm coming. Hold on a little longer.*

And he said, "Will you sing to me?"

And the voice said, *If I can.*

He said, "And will I put my arms around your neck, and will you hold me?"

If you have arms to hold me.

And he knew that he had no arms, and he would have wept bitterly if he could, but he had no tear ducts, no eyes save the sensors that continually fed him data: proximity, acceleration, time till impact.

Still, someone was coming.

Someone who cared.

Perhaps he could be loved again.

Chapter Thirteen

Inside the Dragon

THE DRAGON'S HEAD was a labyrinth. Corridors branched; the walls pulsated, were covered with an oily membrane; a rancid liquid oozed from a million pores. The *dailongzhen* led the landing party farther and farther downward, or at least it seemed downward to Simon Tarses, although his sense of up and down was all askew. Everything proceeded according to some ancient ritual; two of the oarsmen were swinging gilded censers that belched forth sick-sweet fumes; two more held torches aloft, leading the way, pausing now and then to utter incantations as though to allay the dragon's spirit. Simon could not help but be caught up in the exotic rhythm of the ritual. The incense seemed to fill his nostrils; it seemed to intensify the chanting, the clanging of ritual gongs, the garish colors of the *dailong*'s innards. He was getting a headache from the din in his ears.

Only Data was unaffected. Simon watched him as he examined the fleshy walls, at one point even appearing to taste the liquid that was dripping down. "Intriguing," he was saying to himself. "An unusually high silicon content."

Adam, the little boy, was chattering away at Data's side. He seemed quite devoted to the android. Ahead, the boy's father moved purposefully behind the *dailongzhen*. The incense billowed now; there was a kind of wind inside the tunnels here, and Simon could not help but breathe in the fumes. They were making him woozy.

"I'm dizzy," he said as the android stopped to examine another curious feature, an array of tentacular arms that waved delicately back and forth like a sea anemone. "Something in the incense."

"That," said Halliday, "is *gruyesh,* the secret ingredient in the incense. It's mildly hallucinogenic, and an essential adjunct to most of their religious rituals."

"Don't breathe in too much at a time," said Adam. "You can get drunk on the fumes."

Simon had visions of his Romulan ancestors carousing with their drinking vessels brimming with ale.

At length, after descending what seemed to be a spiral staircase made of bone and cartilage, and crossing what seemed to be a rope bridge over a boiling river of bile, they came to an inner chamber.

The strange thing was, the room had a passing resemblance to the bridge of a starship. There were outcroppings of bone, and a central thronelike structure on which the *dailongzhen* sat himself, gripping two of the tentacle-like excrescences in his hands.

"Awaken, O spirit of the deep!" he intoned. The chamber was small and most of the oarsmen were waiting in the corridor that had led here. Only the men with the censers remained, and they stood on either side of the *dailongzhen*, dousing him with the pungent vapors. Adam, Data, Martinez, and Halliday each sat on one of the bony seats; Simon found himself nestled against a cavity in the wall; the flesh gave way, contoured itself to his body, almost as though it were designed that way.

From the corridor beyond came the sound of chanting and the cacophonous jangling of exotic percussion instruments. Then, abruptly, the noise ceased.

The *dailongzhen* stood up. His eyes glowed.

He gripped the tentacles tightly and began to rock back and forth, howling. And around them, images began to form. The ocean. The convoy of skiffs that had pulled up alongside the *dailong*. The crowd of Thanetians, laughing, parading about on the dragon's back, rejoicing as the waves beat against the flanks of the great creature.

"Astonishing," Data whispered. "These are membraneous . . . *viewscreens,* projecting pictures from sensors attached to the outside of the creature. They are made from a mesh of rods and cones—like a human eye—and produce images in reaction to—"

"This *is* like the bridge of a starship," Simon said softly. For, as the *dailongzhen* began to wave his arms, there was movement, and the images in the screens were changing, shifting direction—the *dailongzhen* was steering the sea dragon! A stomach-wrenching turn, and he saw now, they had made a full turn and were heading in the direction of the harbor. He could see, rearing up above the waves, the spires and minarets and twisted towers and diamantine domes, and even, in the misty height, the very palace of the High Shivantak—and the whole image ghostly, fringed with refractive rainbows. They were skimming the ocean's surface now, the *dailong* rapidly contracting and expanding its musculature. Several moons had risen, and their light danced against the purple of setting Klastravo.

"And this," Halliday was explaining, "is how they travel. Short distances, they use little boats, they have canals and artificial waterways, naturally, but—but the wide-open spaces of their world are all water, and these creatures are their ocean liners—guided by telepathic navigators half-drunk on the vapors of *gruyesh*."

And now the *dailongzhen* seemed to have settled into a kind of trance, and the great creature was settling. A deep thrumming permeated the chamber.

"And this," said Halliday, "is one of the profound mysteries of this planet. These creatures—the principal mode of transportation—don't seem to be entirely natural. But the Thanetians didn't build them. No. They rely on ritual hunts to bring in a new beast every time they require another vessel. But the *dailong* are triumphs of bioengineering."

"I bet the answer is right here somewhere," Simon said. "Any ship this complex must have a computer, right? It might not be a computer as we know it, but well, isn't Commander Data living proof that computers don't have to look like computers?"

"I believe you are correct," said Data. "We are within the interior of an extremely large artificial intelligence, and the *dailongzhen* is navigating by means of a human/machine interface, crude but effective. Dr. Halliday, is it permitted for me to attempt to interface with this machine?"

Halliday said, "I don't see why not. *I've* been attempting to interface with one for months, and no one has said I couldn't."

Around them, the rainbow-fringed viewscreens showed vistas of Thanet's oceans; to starboard, the capital city loomed up in front of a setting sun and whirling moons. The *dailongzhen* was fully in control now, and the dragon sailed smoothly; they could see, on one screen, its body stretched out across the sea, with finlike appendages propelling it through the waves. Overhead, a flock of snowy *inari* birds flew in geometric formation that shifted periodically against gathering darkness.

"Those bunches of tentacles," Halliday said, "that

line the walls. As you can see, these people are able to communicate with the *dailong* in some way through them. I've always thought they were some kind of psionic amplifier, and that the *dailongzhen* must have some kind of telepathic talent that can link to the creatures; but perhaps there's a more technological side to it all."

"Is there a location here," asked Data, "with an especially high concentration of the tentacles? A data node, perhaps?"

"Yes," said Halliday. "Behind the control throne, there's usually a passageway that leads to—I've always thought of it as a brain of sorts."

Carefully, Halliday threaded his way through the crowd of celebrants. Absorbed in their chanting, the throng parted for the group and closed up again without missing a beat. Behind the throne, there was a round opening in the wall; a ring of muscle-like flesh encircled it, and they could see a tunnel descending into gloom. Simon noticed that young Adam had pushed his way to the front of the queue; he showed no fear as he led the way into darkness, feeling his way along the dank walls.

In the passageway, they could barely see. "Don't they have any lights in this place?" Adam said.

No sooner had she spoken than the walls began to glow with a faint bluish phosphorescence. The passageway was widening. "It's almost as if—it *understood* you!" Simon said.

"The *dailong* does appear to be conscious of your human thoughts," Data said.

"Not human, maybe," Adam said. "After all, I *am* part Betazoid."

"*Part* is the part we must emphasize here," said Dr. Halliday. "And we're not a hundred percent sure of which part." Father and son laughed.

"And therefore in possession of rudimentary telepathic abilities?" asked Data.

"Really good intuition, at least," Adam's father said.

"Look!" Adam cried. "Down there!"

Sure enough, they could see another of the rainbow-fringed doorways, around which the dragonflesh pulsated and oozed. The belly of the beast, Simon thought, thinking of myths he had heard. The last few yards of the passageway descended steeply, but to his surprise there was a bony flight of steps and even a rail made of a tendonlike material, and the lights brightened. If he hadn't been convinced before that this creature was made by a humanoid species, he certainly was now.

The chamber they found themselves in was completely symmetrical, with a circular wall covered with small tentacles. They were delicate, fibrous strands that glowed an eerie blue and waved back and forth as though immersed in the waters of the sea.

The ceiling was another viewscreen, divided into sections that each seemed to monitor the outside world from a different direction. In the center of the room were raised platforms; as Data, Tormod, and the others reached the platforms, soft tongues of flesh rose up and licked their hands.

"I do believe the creature is trying to locate some kind of input-output port," he said. "Perhaps I should provide some assistance."

Data held out one arm and with his other hand opened up his forearm to reveal a mass of hardware. Simon watched in awe as, snakelike, the tentacles slithered and hissed and found connections inside the commander's body.

"What are you experiencing?" Halliday asked.

"A welter of images—streams, rivers of information," Data said mildly. "It is unquestionably intriguing."

"But what is it you see?" said Halliday. "I've been here for months, trying to find out what makes this planet tick—and you seem to have gotten right through to it in a day."

"I believe," Data said, "that I can make much of this information available to the entire group."

And suddenly the room was whirling. Fumes rose up from the floor—incense, the salt spray of the sea—and images were coalescing out the mist—the floor was buckling—an involuntary cry escaped Simon's throat. Had the *dailongzhen* lost control, was the dragon vessel capsizing? But no—this was a far more familiar kind of disorientation. It was as though this brain chamber were transforming into a holodeck.

And then, all of a sudden, they were on board a

Viking longship, very much like the model Engvig had set up in Simon's quarters.

The sun that beat down on them was more blue than the sun of Earth, and the mountains that jutted up in the distance were of a deep purple hue, and crystalline, but the salt tang of the sea was achingly familiar.

The prow of the ship was carved into the same visage as the *dailong*'s, though now, of course, in miniature. The sea was a different hue, more gray somehow. Lizardfish with tails and fins leaped from the water.

This was a vessel like the skiff they had come on, with chanting oarsmen, all of wood. But Simon and the other members of his party were no longer in their modern clothes—they wore tunics fringed with fur, and to his amazement there was a bronze dirk in his belt, with a handle studded with bright green gemstones. Data was wearing a *dailongzhen*-like costume, with a priestly headdress and a white robe.

"Amazing," said Halliday. "The realism of it—it's every bit as sophisticated as holodeck technology."

"Where are we?" Simon asked. "What are we doing here?"

Data said, "We are in a kind of library—a vast information retrieval system. Apparently, this information has been waiting for us for several thousand years. It is the key to the true history of Thanet."

"But why are we here, where is this?" asked Halliday. "This is a seascape that almost looks like Thanet—but not quite. The sun is wrong, the texture of the sea is subtly different."

"Quite so, Dr. Halliday," Data said. "We're not on Thanet at all. Thanet is not the Thanetians' native planet."

Together, Data and the others began to experience history—a colorful history, a history of trauma and bloodshed—a history that was nothing like the so-called ancient wisdom the Thanetians had received from their sacred texts. . . .

Chapter Fourteen

The Comet's Heart

DEANNA TROI felt the momentary disjuncture of the transporter. In an instant, she materialized inside the comet. She was dizzy. It was the gravity. The corridor she was in corkscrewed up and around and over and the center of gravity didn't seem to be in one place. And then there was the tide of infantile desolation, sweeping over her, threatening to engulf her, drown her—her stomach turned. She reached out for anything, anyone—

And Riker was there, holding her for a moment. She looked into his eyes. Saw the calm center of him, knew that deep within him was the ghost of an old love; she felt it and was comforted. "I'm here, Deanna," he said softly.

The air was thin here, but breathable; the O_2 level

at least seemed tolerable. But the anxiety level was almost unmanageable. Pinpricks of fear and desolation bombarded her. Slowly she got a grip on herself, steadied herself. *All in a day's work for an empath,* she told herself wryly. *If only people knew how much it takes out of you, keeping yourself open like this.*

A dim, sourceless light permeated the passageway. It had a bluish tinge; there was a coldness to it; Deanna shuddered.

"Well," Riker said, "this is artificial all right." He peered around. The walls at first seemed featureless, but as their eyes grew used to the light, she started to see patterns—lines etched into the metallic surface—ancient circuits, perhaps. This was no ordinary passageway. They were inside a machine of some kind, one sophisticated enough to have targeted Thanet—a weapon.

"We're inside," Riker communicated to the bridge.

"Listen," Deanna said.

At first it was a low moaning, almost at the threshold of hearing.

"But there's no wind here," Riker said.

"You sense it," said Deanna. "You, too, Will. So it's more than just an empathic vibration in the air."

The moaning increased in volume. It tugged at her very heartstrings. Within the windlike sighing there was a human voice—the cry of a child. "This comet is alive," she said softly. "More than that—it's sentient."

The sighing crescendoed. Within the windlike wuthering, a child's voice was now clearly audible. Deanna felt a vibration within her soul—that sense of *loss-without-hope-of-retrieval,* as though she had lost an entire race, an entire species, as though she were the last survivor of some planet-smashing holocaust. She knew of only a few beings who lived surrounded by such an aura. She had felt it with Guinan sometimes, had wondered how a person could carry such a weight within themselves and still be so much at peace.

"I guess we should just follow the voice," said Riker.

"Yes."

There was a sensation of falling. The voice was definitely *down;* it came from below, from a place that humans thought of as the abyss—inferno—hell.

Around her, so vivid she could not distinguish reality from illusion, image upon image now—an ocean of fire—screams of dying—cities aflame—a child fleeing through the labyrinthine passageways of a doomed city—columns of a great temple snapping like twigs, roofs caving in, warriors sliced in two by great swaths of laser death. The tunnel became more twisted now, spiraling. They passed through tiny cells like the chambers inside a conch shell.

At length they came to an inner chamber. *A womb,* Deanna thought. It was so narrow that she and Riker could barely squeeze inside. And inside the womb—a child—a boy, Deanna realized, not quite at the age of puberty—a boy who was much too far from home.

Gravity righted itself here, and they found themselves standing before the child as though before an altar. Naked, he floated in a pod of some transparent material, a nutrient fluid bathing him; his eyes were open, but unaware, as though in an unnatural sleep. There were metal tendrils weaving about his feet and hands, and a dozen cyborg connectors sprouted from his shaved head.

His fingers were webbed—this boy was clearly of the same species as the Thanetians. Yet how many parsecs had this comet traversed? There was a mystery here, and Deanna realized that the only way to bring a true resolution to the Thanetians' dilemma was to find the answers.

If only the boy could speak.

And then he did speak, in a way.

You are the one who is not my mother—yet stands in her place, he said.

His lips did not move, but she clearly heard the voice in her mind. Startled, she looked at Riker. He too seemed puzzled.

"I heard a voice," Deanna said.

"And I felt—something," Riker said. "If even I can feel it, I can imagine how it must be affecting you."

Who are you? Deanna called out in her mind.

I am the thanopstru, the voice whispered. She knew the word. It was a Thanetian word, and it meant *bringer of death.* It was the name, in the Sacred Panvivlion, of the destroyer that would come at the end of time.

But this instrument of divine vengeance was supposed to be some terrible force of nature, surely—not a terrified little boy.

Help me, help me, oh help me.

And then, as Deanna gazed on the child's face, feeling his immeasurable torment, she saw a single tear form in his right eye—and slide down his cheek before dissolving into the nutrients that bathed him.

"Of course I will," Deanna whispered. "Of course." She backed up the words with a powerful current of goodwill and affection, drawing on feelings she had known as a child—warmth, love, the protecting arms of a loving parent.

Don't, said the voice within. *No, no, don't tell me those things—they contradict—the program—they violate—the conditioning—they—*And then, a deeper voice, rhythmic, terrifying: *Kill! Kill! Kill! Kill! Kill!*

Part Three:
The Mortal That Was a Machine

There shall come in the last days of the world a Thanopstru, that is to say, a Bringer of Death. And this shall be his sign. He shall shine in the night sky like a sun, yet be tailed like a meteor. Brighter than the dancing moons shall he shine, and the last days will be rich with the rushing of dailong in the seas, and joyous with dancing. Be of good cheer. Ye are doubly blessed, who live in the days of the Thanopstru.

And in moments of terror or hardship, ye shall recite over and over the holy name of the Thanopstru, and from the certain knowledge of the coming cataclysm, you shall draw comfort, you shall find stillness without your troubled hearts.

—From the Holy Panvivlion

ONCE MORE, CAPTAIN PICARD was poring through those field notes, trying to glean some bit of information they could fix on, something to explain the mysteries of Thanet.

And once more, the problems seemed to get more and more convoluted, the more one delved into them.

He looked up: he found himself face-to-face with Guinan. Somehow, she had known he needed to speak with her.

He said, "Look, it's easy to say, don't touch their belief system, don't upset their civilization. But then, I start thinking.

"If a man is dying of an incurable, painful disease—if he's suffering, if science cannot help—and he decides to pull his own plug—that's one ethical dilemma. But if he's in the prime of life, if he has nothing holding him back except an illusion—if he has so much left to give to the rest of the world, so much potential, so much art and literature, so much beauty—is it right to strip away that illusion?"

"Your call, Captain," Guinan said softly.

"I know it is," Picard said, and turned back to Halliday's field notes, feeling once again—

"The aloneness," Guinan sighed. "Yes, I know."

CONFIDENTIAL REPORT:

Dr. Robert Halliday's field notes

The transcript continues:

Last week, I went to a *thanhalyrion,* which is a sort of wake for the end of the world. There was more singing and dancing than you can imagine, and what amazed me was that, within the rigidity of their class structure, there seemed to be more than a little fluidity. There was an intoxicating liquid called *peftifesht* wine, which made everyone very merry but seemed to have the side effect of relaxing the caste system.

At precisely seven minutes after the hour of Karambé Ascendant (the Thanetians measure time by the complex rhythms of their many moons) a beautiful woman—a virgin, I was told—emerged from an inner room into the atrium.

There was a sweeping spiral staircase in the middle of the courtyard that seemed to lead nowhere. The staircase leaned; it ended on a tiny parapet that overlooked the everpresent sea. Well, the celebrants immediately fell into a trancelike state when the virgin entered, and they immediately began to whisper, over and over, like a mantra, the word *thanopstru*. Well, words are just air, but you cannot imagine how terrifying it is to hear this word whispered, in unison, by a hundred people, rhythmically, almost like zombies.

The chanting crescendoed; it was more than a whisper now, it was a thunder-roar, and the young woman mounted the parapet, and suddenly, maybe it was a break in the clouds in the night sky, maybe it was a moment preordained by their astronomers, but there appeared at the zenith of heaven this glowing, many-tailed star—a comet, I suppose—and the virgin leaped into the sea.

And then the chanting stopped, and there was silence for a very long time as everyone at the party drank an entire goblet of *peftifesht*— and another, and another—while I, an alien and a xenoanthropologist, eager to etch every moment of this bizarre ritual onto the clay tablets of my consciousness, did not drink, and was perhaps the only halfway sober person in the entire courtyard.

Here's the strangest part: I know the girl jumped. I saw her dive, heard the splash when she hit the waves. Yet an hour later, when I asked the other witnesses how they felt about the death of one so young, they denied the whole incident! Indeed, there was such a legend of a virgin suicide in their mythology. A beautiful story, they said, but it was of the past, not the present. And, they assured me, it was fiction, not fact.

The Thanetians live in a world that in their own minds is fleeting, illusory; they do not believe that the real is real. This is in conflict with the Federation which is, on the whole, materialistic; the spiritual is often kept to one side. So, for all I know, nobody saw a young woman leap to her death. For all I know, they all edited it out of their collective thoughts; we need to have this *peftifesht* analyzed; I will include a sample in my next physical reports package—assuming the planet is still here in a month.

I think I actually will *down* a goblet of that *peftifesht* before I start on the next chapter of these field notes.

"Computer," said the captain, "what's *in* the *peftifesht?*"

"Water, mostly," said the computer. "Water, simple carbohydrates, a few trace elements."

"Nothing that would get anyone drunk," Picard said, thinking of the vineyards of his childhood home—lost now, lost.

So even their native intoxicant worked by the magic of illusion, of autosuggestion. Culture was the primary imperative, not chemistry. The mind was master, not the world beyond.

He took a sip of the synthetic *peftifesht*. It was cool, a little cloying—and not intoxicating in the slightest.

Chapter Fifteen

To Save a World

"HE HAS SO MUCH to tell us," Deanna said, back on the *Enterprise*. "I have to go back in. There *has* to be a way to save him."

In the conference room, the atmosphere was serious. There was a profound conflict here; the Federation had standard rules for adjudicating such conflicts, yet these were sentient beings—a few *million* sentient beings—whose civilization and self-image were at stake.

Picard had agreed to let the ambassador and his daughter sit in on the meeting. The hours, of course, were ticking away. It seemed only minutes ago that they still had two days to figure out what to do. Now it was down to a few hours. He had sent in technicians—he hadn't dared risk sending Troi in again yet—and finally the ship's doctor.

"Dr. Crusher?" Picard turned to Beverly, who had just made a brief trip to the comet's heart, and who now appeared somber and dejected.

She said, "I've analysed the boy's cell structure, the hard-wiring of his neurons to the silicon-based nervous system of the comet itself—and I've got to tell you, there's no way to free him. His brain has been soldered into the computer that runs that infernal weapon. It's appalling."

Picard watched the ambassador, whose fists clenched and unclenched on the table. *What he must be going through,* he thought. *It's all unraveling—everything he ever held to be ultimate truth.* "You're saying that to remove the boy from the weapon would be—"

"To kill him, Captain," said Dr. Crusher.

"And yet," said the captain, "the needs of the many—" He was quoting the ancient adage that a great hero of the Federation had once uttered, giving his life for the life of his ship—all knew those words by heart, and all honored them.

"It's true," said Worf. "Yet honor demands that we exhaust all possibilities before allowing death to occur needlessly—"

Picard said, "Mr. La Forge?"

"Beverly is right, Captain," La Forge said. "We can't separate the boy from the comet without severing vital neural links. He's part of that thing now, a cyborg as it were."

Picard shuddered, remembering a time when he too had been joined to a great machine—a machine intent on destroying all individuality, all true sentience in the entire galaxy.

"But we'd just be *killing* him," said Counselor Troi, and Picard understood that she, of all the crew members, had actually felt what the comet felt, had been one with its emotions.

"As he would kill millions of others," Picard said, with relentless logic.

"Captain, there's a margin of safety still. An hour, half an hour—to find out what we need to know. We don't know what world this comet is from or why the boy welded to the machine is so clearly Thanetian in species. We ought to know these things."

Before we destroy him, Picard added silently. He winced. Perhaps the child's death was inevitable, but he would be damned if he wouldn't use every resource and every moment at his disposal to change the boy's fate.

La Forge spoke up suddenly. "Captain, Commander Data is contacting us from the planet's surface—just beneath the surface, actually."

"On screen," said the captain.

Data's face formed where there had been a sea of stars. He was seated—no, *enveloped*—in a chair that seemed to be made of flesh, with tentacles writhing about his arms and feet. Behind him, other members of the *Enterprise* away team, as well as Dr. Halliday and his son, seemed similarly tethered to a wall. The room resembled an organic version of a control room in a starship.

"Captain," said Data, "the largest fauna on this world are not natural creatures at all. They are some kind of elaborately bioengineered cyborg, and they seem to contain records, racial memories, of Thanet's history beyond the five thousand years the Thanetians have themselves recorded. It seems they have been expecting us—or someone, at any rate. This technology parallels the holodeck technology, except that the neurons fired are of living tissue rather than inorganic in origin."

The bridge crew looked at their comrade on the screen, and then at each other, in wonder.

"Captain, I believe we are on the verge of understanding why this *thanopstru* has been launched to destroy Thanet. I am assimilating information as quickly as my positronic brain paths will permit. A few more hours ought to illuminate everything. There seems to be—some kind of communication between the *dailong* and the comet—one is controlling the other—it is uncertain which. We are seeing the past right now. With astonishing verisimilitude. We were wrong about this world in many ways. It is not primitive at all. In fact, we are sensing the biography of the very life-form inside the comet now—and we are living through a simulacrum of its actual lifetime, five thousand years ago."

"I knew nothing of this!" said the ambassador. "Does the High Shivantak perhaps know something we do not know? Is our entire culture—an artificial construct?"

Suddenly the ambassador's daughter spoke up. "Counselor, perhaps you will have need of—someone who understands the Thanetian language and culture. I think I should go with you. When I was younger, I trained with the *dailongzhen* of my community, hoping that I would one day catch and navigate a *dailong* myself—it's the only way a Thanetian can ever transcend the limitations of caste. I don't have *much* telepathic ability, but I could probably—help you with a few concepts."

"The inner chamber is very cramped," Picard said.

"This is *our* history you're unearthing. One of us needs to be there. If we didn't have a say in our past, and may not have one in our future," Kio said with passion, "we should at least know what's going on."

Beverly Crusher said, "I *could* monitor her life signs remotely, and give the order to have her evacuated from on board the *Enterprise*."

He could have said no. Maybe he should have. But if the girl's own father, so overprotective when it came to an innocent romance, was willing to let her risk her life for knowledge, who was Picard to stand in the way?

"Make it so," said Captain Picard, sighing.

Chapter Sixteen

Tanith

LANDFALL NOW. Not Thanet. Another world. The longship was pulling ashore next to a gilded pagoda guarded by ten-story demons of stone. They were docking—and Simon Tarses seemed to know what he was doing, Data observed, as he tugged at the ropes and made the sail fold up. The ancient technology was fascinating, mixed as it was with what seemed almost anachronistic, a sky busy with personal flying craft and larger rocket ships, and what looked like an artificial moon with blinking lights that spelled out commercial messages in an alien tongue which Data was already devoting a small part of his brain to deciphering.

As Commander Data walked through the ship from stern to prow, it occurred to him that no one could see him. They were looking right through him, these people, Thanetian in somatype even though they appeared to be on a different world. Yet it was different with Tarses, Dr. Halliday, Adam, and Lieutenant Martinez. They were moving among the sailors, smiling, chatting away in some native tongue. He had almost completed the decipherment of it, comparing it with millions of known language paradigms; his positronic brain was parsing, analyzing, breaking down phonemes, and reassembling the components of this language almost at the speed of light. Soon, bits of it were making sense.

There were two layers of reality here; though he was perceiving this simulacrum all about him, he was also in communication with the bridge of the *Enterprise.*

In one compartment of his mind, then, he was aware that Deanna Troi and the daughter of Ambassador Straun were preparing to board the *thanopstru,* and that they would soon be entering, in some way, the comet's consciousness, which was linked through subspace to the great databases within the *dailong.*

Two of the Federation's party seemed vaguely aware of his presence.

"Adam?" he said. "Lieutenant Tarses?"

The boy stopped. He appeared frightened.

"What's wrong, Artas?" Simon said.

"Nothing, Indhuon," said the boy. "It's just that—I think I just saw a ghost."

The names—and they were speaking the dialect

of this world. Data realized that the crew members had assumed roles in this ancient drama, and that they were perhaps only subliminally conscious of their own identities. Each was a hitchhiker inside an ancient soul. Data supposed that, as an android, he must be exempt from this.

Or was each of the crew members experiencing this show differently—was each of the members aware of himself, yet unable to communicate with the *Enterprise* members inhabiting other bodies?

He decided to continue gathering data.

"Captain," he said—no one reacted to the strange phenomenon of an alien creature touching a chest device and addressing the empty air—"we are on another planet. In a civilization somehow parallel with Thanet's but not entirely congruent with it."

La Forge's voice now in response: "Can you transmit any relevant data on the planet? Positions of stars and moons in the sky?"

"Yes," Data said. "Though I am subjectively experiencing this other world, I know that I am still actually interfacing with the *dailong*'s central nervous system. I should be able to access its databanks and fill you in."

The boy that looked like Adam continued to stare at Data.

"Hush," said Tarses-Indhuon, "there's no one. Come."

"Are you a ghost?" the boy said.

The wind was stirring as the boat was being

moored to the dock. Silently and efficiently, the crew began to file out into the harbor. And such a harbor it was! Boats shaped like a hundred mythical creatures plied the waters. A golden dome peered above the waves, and now and then, from one of a dozen mouthlike openings, a spacecraft would emerge; their ships were shaped like spiders, or butterflies with delicate, spindlelike antennae. There was a sunset—no, two sunsets—no, Data realized, the bloated, purplish sun was setting, the darker dwarf was rising; this was a world that survived precariously within the complex dance of a double star.

"I am not a ghost," said Data softly.

"Come away, little one," said the one who seemed to be Simon Tarses. "You're talking to the wind again."

"I am not the wind," Data said. But he became aware that there was a susurrant undertone to his voice as it emerged from his artificial larynx, and that perhaps it might seem to be the whispering of the breeze.

The Tarses-simulacrum blinked for a moment, as if not sure whether he heard something. But he soon seemed to dismiss what he might have heard.

Adam said, "But you know I can see things other people can't see. That's why I was picked for the *dailong* training program."

"And you are doing well at it," said Lisa Martinez, who was wearing the flowing robes of a *dailongzhen*. "I think that there won't be any problem progressing to the semifinals—an amazing find for someone so young! Your mother and sister will be so proud."

They stepped onto dry land now. Everything around them was similar to, yet subtly different from, the world of Thanet. The rigid hierarchy was in place, Data noticed; everywhere there were caste garments, and some made automatic deference to others of superior standing.

He heard the voice of La Forge now, echoing unnoticed in the air around him. "We've located the planet," he said. "Well—what's left of it, anyway."

"Tanith," came the voice of Dr. Beverly Crusher.

At that point, Dr. Halliday emerged onto the dock. He was wearing the most elaborate robes of all, and a headdress of monumental proportions. How appropriate that he had been incarnated here as so gaudy a specimen!

Data continued his communication with the *Enterprise*. "We have all assumed the roles of historic personages," he said. "Except for myself; I appear to have become a ghost."

The Adam-child, who was the only one who seemed to hear anything of Data's utterances, said, "I always knew this ship was haunted."

Then there was another voice, echoing in his head: "This is better than the wooden roller coaster at the Academy's museum of ancient amusements!"

"You *can* hear me, Adam!" Data said.

"There's a bit of me inside this other kid—his name is Artas. The bit that is my Adam-consciousness can communicate with you—and you can report what I see back to the *Enterprise*. I guess you're the all-purpose interface around here, Data."

The voice of Dr. Robert Halliday then reverberated in Data's mind, confirming Adam's assumption. "Apparently, I am inhabiting the body of one of the great sages of ancient Tanith, a man named Hal-Therion sar-Bensu. He is a distant relation of Ambassador Straun."

"A relation?" Data asked. "But surely these are two different planets."

"Different the way two zygotes split from one might be? The worlds were sisters once. And as close relations often do, they fought. Bitterly and unrelentingly, for tens of thousands of years."

Starcraft were being launched from the golden dome that reared up from the heart of the city. He realized that almost all of the ships were aimed at a single coordinate.

Thanet.

On the bridge, a welter of information and images was being relayed as Captain Picard watched, and his crew analyzed.

Tanith was a beautiful world and, apart from its strange orbit around a double-star system, could have been the twin of Thanet. But Tanith's civilization was no more. Images of wasteland came flooding in from the ship's computer as it verified Data's coordinates.

There were mountains sheared into plateaus.

Pockmarks of bombardments. Tanith's atmosphere, once rich in oxygen, had become a soup of poisons. And the destruction was clearly man-made. Tanith's death had been caused by a hail of comets—comets just like the one that was now heading toward Thanet. Comets that contained many types of destructive weapons, from primitive thermonuclear devices to viruses to the biological wherewithal for a kind of reverse terraforming—the metamorphosis of a friendly world into an uninhabitable deathworld.

The horror of the present contrasted with the images that were being gleaned from Data's transmission and which were appearing on screen. They were not images of the pinpoint clarity that would be produced by a Federation computer, but blurred sometimes, and sometimes fringed with a prismatic field; the mechanisms of image retrieval and transmission were clearly quite alien, and had the flavor of a biological origin.

Meanwhile, there was Deanna Troi. She and the girl had already beamed aboard the comet, and a third series of images was being transmitted now, so that the bridge's viewing area was now a jigsaw puzzle, the pictures complementing each other, contradicting each other too, sometimes.

Picard watched as Deanna and Kio inched their way down the narrow corridor, their footsteps spiraling with the changing gravity. There was something about those walkways that reminded him of his own subjugation to the Borg—the dehumanizing horror of it lived inside him, would always be with him.

Even in his dreams of childhood, the idyllic vineyards of his youth, there was always a machine. Watching. Never letting go. *What that child must be going through,* Picard thought.

The innermost chamber irised open, and he saw the child.

I cannot weep. I cannot feel. I have no eyes. I have no limbs.

But I see eyes. But I see limbs.

They do not exist.

I see a young boy floating. I see limbs. I see eyes. I see a tear roll down his cheek. Isn't that you?

Limbs? Eyes? Flesh is an illusion.

Deanna wept.

Data watched the sailors say their good-byes and leave the pier. A robot, hovering in the air, sang military slogans as it swam past them, passing out flyers that appeared to advertise a military draft.

Thanetians are your foes, the robot sang. *The only good Thanetian is a dead Thanetian.*

He found that with a bit of selective bank switching, he was able to read the thoughts of those characters in the drama whose bodies were also inhabited by the *Enterprise* crew members from the distant future and the members of the research team—Adam, Tarses, Halliday, and all the others were functioning as a sort of mirroring algorithm, allowing the information expressed in the form of human thoughts to be read as word-based data.

Now he was in Artas's mind:

Gotta hurry home. Where's Mother? The big day coming soon. So much excitement. So much riding on it all. Don't want to disappoint her. . . .

Hal-Therion sar-Bensu:

Danger to the world. The boy is our great hope—perhaps our greatest.

She was standing by the water's edge, blowing the boy a kiss, a beautiful dark-haired woman with curiously intense eyes—

"Mother!" Artas cried out.

Data's gaze followed the boy. His mother, he realized, was being played in this simulation by another member of the *Enterprise*.

Artas ran through the crowd into the arms of Counselor Deanna Troi, laughing as she embraced him.

A young girl stood beside Deanna, a girl with the face of Kio sar-Bensu; behind her, three fierce-looking women stood guard. She was watching the longship intently, waiting for someone. When Indhuon appeared behind his younger brother, she waved at him; but he averted his eyes.

"I'm in," Deanna said, "and seeing the ancient planet through the eyes of—the boy's mother. Appropriate enough."

Picard listened, and behind him the ambassador sat, consternation written all over his face as the multitasking viewscreens alternated between the viewpoints of various characters, all the images linked through the central conduit of Data's mind. It was almost as though Data's consciousness was editing the raw footage of these people's lives into a continuous story with all the excitement of a well-written holodeck program. The other crew members, too, sat riveted by the story.

"Now *I'm* in," came Kio sar-Bensu's excited voice. "Oh—this is beautiful—like a dream version of our world."

"Witchcraft! Heresy!" the ambassador muttered.

"I'm someone very important here," Kio continued. "This woman here is the mother of Artas, a boy everyone is calling 'The Great Hope.' But even she defers to me. And my father is—look, there he comes!"

They saw him on screen now—wearing the face and somatype of Dr. Robert Halliday, but the robes of a very high official indeed—

"A Shivan-Jalar!" the ambassador gasped. "They exist only in our mythology—why, the High Shivantak himself communicates with the spirit of one, within the holiest of holies, which only he can enter."

"So Thanet had a sister world once, a planet not too far away, who shared its culture," Picard said.

La Forge continued to report the results of his research. "Tanith," he said, "doesn't exist. What's left is uninhabitable. The atmosphere is stripped away mostly, what's left is poisonous gases, the oceans evaporated, the continents pockmarked—I'll put it on screen."

A collage of a devastated planet appeared next to the lush image of the seaport.

"Can that really be the same world?" Picard said.

"If those coordinates are accurate—or even relatively accurate," La Forge said. "There's no other world, dead or alive, that falls into that range."

Ambassador Straun was struggling to frame a question. "H-How—long ago—are the images we're seeing?"

"The ruined world is now, Your Excellency," La Forge said. "The living images you're seeing are—five thousand or so years—I can get an exact fix based on the positions of key stars in the simulated evening sky—five thousand point zero seven years old."

It hit them all at once. Picard saw that they all knew it. No one had to say it aloud.

The people in those images had only a few days to live.

Chapter Seventeen

Angels

ARTAS AWOKE. Today was the day he'd been waiting for. He was the fastest, the brightest. He had passed the penultimate test, and there was only one remaining.

I am the one, he thought, *who will redeem my people.*

Tanith's striated sunlight streamed in through the screens. He rubbed his eyes. *Yesterday was wonderful,* he thought. *I rode in the Great* Shivan-Jalar's *private barge. His Multitude actually smiled at me—actually shared with me a piece of his private candy!* He sat up, looked at himself in the mirror-pool at the foot of his bed, preening in front of his image. He was twelve years old, and by the end of the day he hoped to win a great prize—the privilege of never seeing his thirteenth birthday.

Then—something strange happened.

The mirror pool began to shift and swirl. A kind of smoke started spiraling from it, and the reflective mirrorstuff started shimmering. Grumbling, he reached down to see if he could adjust the settings.

And then, suddenly, there was another boy in the room, stepping out of the mirror pool. He wore alien clothing, no tunic but a double-legged second skin that hugged his legs, and an upper covering of the same stretch fabric. Embarrassed that he was not yet dressed, Artas quickly donned his tunic, with its clan markings, which told everyone who he was and let those who must defer to him know their place.

The alien boy had no clan markings at all.

"What are you doing here?" he said.

The boy's lips moved, but nothing came out. He seemed to be struggling with a shiny handheld device. His hands were not webbed.

"Is this the final test that I'm supposed to undergo?" Artas asked.

No answer.

"Are you a haunting, sent by one of my rivals?" Again, no response. Artas knew that many of the boys he grew up with were now his enemies, so coveted was the position of great *thanopstru*.

"Finally!" the other boy said. "I got a fix on the translation. This dialect of yours *is* Thanetian, but it's a very ancient form. I couldn't get it to congruency right away."

"You're a Thanetian?" Artas gaped. This was the ultimate horror—the enemy materializing in his very bedroom on the day of the final test!

"No, no. I'm Adam Halliday. I—"

Artas flung himself at the stranger, pummeling him with all the strength his boyish frame could muster. But there was nothing there—the alien boy was insubstantial. Artas found himself banging his fist against the wall.

"Are you all right, Artas?" came a voice. His mother.

Adam put a finger to his lips.

"I—I think so, Mother," the boy said.

"I come from the Federation," said Adam.

"You're just a dream, a figment of my imagination. They said I would dream dreams. It's in the Panvivlion, you know. Why am I telling you this? The Panvivlion probably sent you. You're my quest vision. Naturally. I've got the race this afternoon."

"No, listen," Adam said. "I'm a tourist, sort of. I'm eavesdropping on you, five thousand years in the future. You've already become the great *thanopstru* and—"

"So I will win the race?" Artas could hardly contain his excitement. "I'll be chosen? Everyone tells me I will, but—"

"C'mon, Artas," Adam said. "Listen. A bunch of us are watching your world through your eyes and the eyes of people around us. But no one here knows it. It's a computer simulation that approximates reality—I think. But this old Tanithian technology's pretty advanced, so I don't know whether what I'm seeing is *really* happening or if it's really well simulated. Thing is, no one except you can see any of us."

"Why are you here?"

"I don't know. Because I can't help it. I'm sitting up here in a holodeck sort of a chamber inside a mechanical sea dragon, and I'm watching all this stuff happen to you people, and I just had to reach out. I don't want you to die. Look, I'm having the same problems as you up here in the far future. I have this strong intuition thing that scares off everyone—except that android guy I met a day or two ago, he's hard to scare 'cause he doesn't have any emotions at all. You're kind of like me. And you're going to throw away your life."

Artas suddenly knew who this person was. He shuddered. "You're Saraniu," he said. "The tempter." Artas thought of calling Indhuon, sleeping only a room divider away, but did not want to wake his brother, who had important things of his own to think about.

"Think, Artas!" Adam cried. "I'm a kid like you, and I know what it's like to be different, to be lonely. Look, if I was working for the Federation I wouldn't be talking to you like this—I'd have to follow the Prime Directive, I couldn't tell you anything about my world, my future—"

He was speaking in riddles again. This was a nonsensical vision, something you'd get from downing too much *peftifesht* wine.

"Go away," Artas said.

The image was suddenly gone, and the boy was gazing once more at his own reflection.

Taruna es-Sarion was on the verge of tears; she had often felt like crying in the past few days. She was proud of her son, of course, but she also knew that before he was sent into the sky in glory to wreak the ultimate vengeance on the Thanetians, he would first have to—

Enter the deviving chamber.

That was how the priests referred to it. *The deviving chamber.* Artas would have his life functions, one by one, turned off. Finally, only the brain would be functioning, and its neurons would be fused into the artificial nervous system of the *thanopstru.*

And her son would become more than just a person—he would become the savior of the world.

Artas walked into the dining area of the small living quarters they shared on the four hundredth floor of the prostitutes' quarter of the city. How frail he seemed. In an hour would come the final test. She knew he would win, he *had* to win—but at the same time she hoped against hope that he would fail.

"Do you want to eat, son?" she asked him.

Her other son, Indhuon, was still resting; but he too would have important work to do, if Artas won the position of *thanopstru.* Indhuon would be one of the last people with whom Artas would interact, as he descended into the cylinder of devivement in order to become one with the Deathbringer.

He nodded. She poured him a helping of the thin gruel and crushed bread that was the prescribed morning meal for a son of a woman of the pleasure caste, a woman who had no prospects in life unless her offspring could attain admission to the guild of weaponry—and great prospects if her son had the gifts that could elevate him to the status of *thanopstru,* the star of death.

So much terror, so much hope tied up in this one frail child—she resisted the impulse to hug him hard to her, to crush him against her body; she knew that he would not want that today. He needed to think of otherworldly things, to ready his mind for the great test.

They looked at each other, mother and son.

And then she couldn't resist any more. She took him in her arms. He did not resist, but part of him seemed aloof. She did not weep, and nor did he, but she knew they were both clenching back tears.

Then it happened.

Looking out of the high window, over the sparkling bay whose water glittered in the twin sunlight, she saw a mist form—swirl—condense into the shape of a woman. A woman in a strange, mannish uniform, without a single caste-mark at all, unless it was that peculiar emblem on her breast.

How was she floating there? There was no balcony.

Taruna was about to speak, but the alien put a finger on her lips.

"I'm not really here," she said. "The boy cannot see me. I'm just a voice inside your mind, a voice from the future."

"Are you a—" Taruna hesitated to use the word *angel*. Angels belonged to an ancient past. "Are you a messenger?" she asked.

"No," she said. "I am only here to observe."

"A guardian angel," Taruna whispered. "One who watches."

"I didn't mean to intrude. I'm just a series of neural impulses that somehow managed to skip through subspace into your mind—I'll try to hide. I was released because of the flood of emotion when you—when you hugged Artas."

"Who, what are you?"

"I am Counselor Deanna Troi," she said. She was strangely beautiful, with her ringlets of dark hair and her—unwebbed hands—a sure sign that she was not of this world.

"What caste is Counselor?" Taruna said in her mind, bewildered. "I do not understand."

Troi said, "You love him so much. Don't stop loving him. Your love is what I felt, anchoring him to the real world, when I stood in the dark chamber at the heart of the comet and saw your son—"

"You saw him? In a vision?"

"No—in the flesh—" and Taruna saw, with aching clarity, a vision of her son, naked, frail, floating in a nutrient liquid behind a clear wall—and a single tear welling up in one eye—and all around him machines, cold and dead—and though she had always known what the heart of a *thanopstru* must contain, she had never seen it, could never have seen it—a terrible grief stabbed at her.

"I wish I could stop history," said the woman who called herself *Counselor*. "But in your world I'm only a ghost—I have no reality at all."

"You're a devil creature, a tempter, I know it now," Taruna said. "Don't tell me you saw my son in a living death—he's about to step through the paradise gate, he's about to save us all, he's going to be a martyr, he's going to be reborn as an angel.

"Artashki," she whispered, using his baby name. She thought he would wince, but instead he came back into her arms.

"I want to hear the song again," he said.

She knew at once what song it was—the lullaby she had once sung to him each night, so he would go to sleep and she could go off on her night rounds, the profession that those of her caste practiced.

Sleep, my baby, sleep,
And tomorrow I'll bring you a copper ring
And the next day I'll bring you a silver chain
And the third day I'll bring you a crown of gold.
Sleep, my baby, sleep,
And I'll pluck the twin suns for your eyes
And the twenty moons for your fingers and toes.

By the gods of death, she loved this child.

His eyes were closed. She wondered if he was feigning slumber—a last effort to remain a child, perhaps, knowing that from today he would no longer be one, even if he lost the race.

Oh, you are beautiful, Taruna es-Sarion thought, and wondered what the boy's father was doing; they could not, of course, have anything like an exchange of letters, or even be seen to recognize one another in the street; such things were forbidden between one as exalted as he and a mere woman of the streets.

If only.

"Counselor Troi! Counselor Troi!" It was the voice of Dr. Crusher echoing through her skull. "You slipped out of focus for a moment—your life signs—"

Yes, Deanna thought. *Step back.* The wave of empathic vibration had almost sucked her in, had made her seem to—*participate*—in the simulated past. Or had that meeting with the boy's mother really occurred? At what point did the *dailong*'s virtual creation cross over into actual real history? *Mustn't let the welter of emotions get to me*—

"There," came Beverly's voice again. Now she knew that it was coming from the *Enterprise,* and that she and Kio sar-Bensu were still in the inner chamber of the comet, linked somehow to the mind of this boy and to a moment in ancient history.

"Troi here. I'm fine. I'm going back in."

"Are you sure?"

"I saw into that woman's heart," Troi said. "I want to see it through."

Troi closed her eyes. Suddenly she was in the great plaza of Tanith's capital city, making her way toward the first of many tiers of parapets, packed with citizens chanting slogans.

Chapter Eighteen

The Race

ARTAS LET GO of his mother's hand as soon as they reached the first of seven parapets, representative of the Seven Ages of the Universe. He did not want to appear to be a mama's boy now, not with the fate of the world perhaps resting on his shoulders. Especially not in front of his big brother.

On the parapet were gathered thousands of men, women, and children, all wearing the corona of hatred in their hair, all waving the red-bordered flags of destruction which the city government had been handing out that morning.

A chorus leader whipped up the chanting:

Whom do we despise?
Thanet! Thanet!

Why are they our enemies?
Killers of babies! Slaughterers of the innocent!
How long shall we hate them?
Forever! Forever!

Glittering on the seventh parapet, on a plinth of gold and diamantine, sat the vessel itself, a perfect sphere of shiny silvery metal. Soon the winner of the final test would shed his mortal body and become the soul of the great sphere, and be winging its way toward the enemy.

Artas could barely contain himself. Only for a split second did he look back at his mother, who looked away and did not meet his gaze.

On the third parapet, the place of the High Priests, the Shivan-Jalar sat enthroned on the back of the skeleton of a megamarton, its tusks upraised and holding up a flaming red banner with the sigils of the High Castes of Tanith. His daughter, Ariela, sat beside him, taking notes on his august words, whispering them into a palm device; the device, as it happened, contained the consciousness of Commander Data, who was still the interface between past and future, transmitting information and images back to the *Enterprise*.

From the parapet, the Shivan-Jalar could hear the tumult below, could feel the force of the people's emotion. That force was a powerful thing—if only— if only emotion alone could bring the war to an end, could force the final destruction of Thanet!

The counselors who sat around him, on their various lesser thrones, were stiff, impassive, all awaiting his word. Then the Shivan-Jalar smiled a little, and everyone seemed to relax.

My father, Ariela thought, *more powerful than anyone in the world—even his smiles are watched, analyzed.*

"If only you had been with me on the longship, my daughter," said the Shivan-Jalar. "There was a young navigator—a wonderful match for you, I think. One Indhuon es-Sarion—yes, yes, I know the mother is a whore, but the brother, I understand, is a prime candidate for *thanopstru.*"

"Really, Father," said Ariela, "I do have the right to seek my own mate."

The counselors looked discreetly away, not wishing to intrude on a moment of domestic strain.

Her father clapped his hands.

"Sire," said the first minister, lifting his censer up and wafting a powerful woody perfume over his master's nostrils, "the hour is ripe; perhaps we should proceed to the final test?"

"In time. A thousand years ago—" His Transcendence rose up, placed his palms upward in the gesture known as *drawing-wisdom-from-the-sky.* "—my ancestor undoubtedly sat on such a parapet, meditating on the very purpose of his existence. This time it's different—this time it's the very end of the Thanetian civilization, the final annihilation of those we have been taught for millennia to hate and fear. I think that it's only appropriate for me to ask aloud the question that I know has tormented all of you from time to time, which you do not dare utter for fear of a heresy trial.

"The question, my wise friends," he continued, "is why? Why are we fighting a race that appears to be exactly like us?"

Everyone looked very uncomfortable, and even Ariela wondered whether her father was going too far in testing the limits of the counselors' orthodoxy.

The Shivan-Jalar smiled. "I will tell you the answer today," he said, "on the eve of our victory, which may also be our defeat, for if the Thanetians have not spent the last millennium developing weapons as powerful as ours, I would be most surprised. The answer to that burning question that flirts with heresy, my friends, is that we are all fools. I've prayed on this, I've downed the *zul* potion in almost lethal concentrations in order to communicate with our ancestors, and I've come to the realization that none of this was necessary."

The first counselor, the one who had said it had always been so, said, "Your Transcendence, for the Shivan-Jalar to speak heresy is unthinkable, because you embody orthodoxy in your very person. And yet—"

"Speak your mind, Japthek, you may never get another chance."

"Sire, I've often thought that perhaps the gods . . . are simply toying with us—they've created this duality between two worlds, five thousand years apart in space travel, though only instants away from each other by subspace communication—in order to test some theorem about balance and imbalance."

"Interesting," said Hal-Therion. "So your way out of the Unspeakable Dilemma is—that we are but playthings of destiny. Anyone else?"

"I think," said the second counselor, clearing his throat, "that whatever Your Transcendence says must be the truth; for does not the Panvivlion state that 'the lips of the Shivan-Jalar are the lips of God'?"

"Even I do not know if that is so," said the Shivan-Jalar, "and really, *I* ought to know."

"But if His Transcendence actually *doubted*—"

"I think that's what I'm trying to say, old man," said the sage. And Ariela suddenly realized that her father was not joking after all. "Now, today, on the eve of *everything*—I find myself wrestling with heresy."

"Your Transcendence, even the legendary Tarsu of Salerion struggled with the dark forces before coming face-to-face with the shining hardness of truth," said the first counselor in whining, solicitous tones.

"Silence! I have said the unsayable—now, all of you, do your duty!"

Ariela was paying full attention now. Her father was challenging the others—a challenge that might in ancient times have been met with mortal combat, but that today tended to end more with a wager and a forfeiture of a token payment. Would anyone take the bait?

"Go ahead," Hal-Therion said. "Depose me."

The counselors rose up. This was serious! Such a move could delay everything, cause chaos in the governance of the planet, even prevent the choosing of the *thanopstru!* She could see them all thinking hard now, wondering whether this was their chance to seize power—as her father had once himself done—or whether it was an elaborate bluff, a test of loyalty. Last time, after such a test, the purge of the priestly ranks had lasted weeks, and several hundred had met their end in the auto-da-fé of glory. Ariela knew she must act quickly to defend her father's position—and her own.

She rose to her feet. "No, counselors!" she cried. And in the singsong voice that was used to recite verses from the ancient religious texts, she quoted: "Always, on the brink of the shift in the cycle of the times, there will be a moment of wavering—a time when all possibilities seem equally possible. Do not hesitate to choose the path of death, for the end is ever the gateway to the beginning."

"Well spoken, Ariela sar-Bensu!" said the wheedling Japthek. "You have returned us all to reality with a single well-chosen sacred text."

The moment of tension passed as the counselors sat back down. But when she met her father's gaze, she saw in his eyes a kind of imploring, a desperation: it was as if he was saying to her, amid all this pomp, dressed as he was in robes and feathers and furs and precious metals and all the panoply of a god-on-earth, "Please, daughter, let this cup be taken from me." And Ariela wept, but inside, for sorrow was an emotion that dared not show its face on this, the happiest of days.

"Look!" she said, changing the subject abruptly. "The race has begun!" And she pointed down toward the second and third parapets.

"I can't watch anymore!" Ambassador Straun shouted. "Shivan-Jalars professing heresy, some obscene mirror planet I've never even heard of locked in a fratricidal war with my own world—it's all trickery!"

He stormed from the bridge; concerned, Captain Picard took a moment to go after him personally. After asking the ship's computer, he located the man pacing about in an empty corridor.

Quietly, leaning against a bare wall, the ambassador was weeping.

Gently, Picard touched him on the shoulder. "Courage, Your Excellency," he said softly. "We must play this thing through till the end."

"If this is truth, why could I not have lived a lie?"

"We all want truth, Mr. Ambassador. And sometimes the truth comes with . . . pain that seems unbearable. Come, sir. Let's put a good face on it all, no matter what we learn."

"You don't understand."

"On the contrary," said Picard, "I do understand. Perfectly." Picard thought of the Borg. Something in his eyes must have convinced the ambassador.

The ambassador allowed himself to be led back. Picard had a glass of *peftifesht* wine replicated for him; the ambassador downed it in one gulp, without even worrying whether it had been correctly brewed for a member of his caste.

Grimly, they continued watching.

Indhuon es-Sarion was summoned up to the transcendent parapet level, a place of crystal pennants and peacock thrones. He did not want to meet the gaze of any of the high counselors, all of whom belonged to immeasurably higher castes than did he himself. But the daughter was a different matter. She sat at the foot of her father's throne, her fingers darting nimbly over a handheld device on which she was recording— what? Great matters of state, no doubt. And she was a striking girl, no older, perhaps, than Indhuon himself.

And inside Indhuon's mind, a passenger sat— Lieutenant Simon Tarses, equally entranced by the daughter of the Shivan-Jalar, who seemed the very incarnation of Kio sar-Bensu.

Kio! he called out in his mind before he could stop himself.

To his amazement, a gentle voice whispered in his thoughts. *Simon,* it said, *fancy meeting you here— five thousand years from home, and who knows how many parsecs.*

How is it that we're talking? he thought.

The gentle voice of Commander Data explained the interface.

I thought we'd never meet again, Kio said. *I thought—and then—so much is happening now—* The voice died away.

I am sorry, Data said. *There is only a finite amount of data I can process, and my highest priority is communicating to the* Enterprise. *So any other exchanges will have to remain on a lower priority for now.*

The *Enterprise* was Simon's highest priority too—or it should be, he chided himself. It would be, he determined. He would just have to put Kio out of his mind and concentrate on his duties, which at the moment seemed to involve watching an amazing spectacle through this Indhuon person's eyes. *As assignments go, it's not too bad,* he thought. Crowded parapets stretched below him arrayed according to the major caste divisions, with the priestly ones here at the very top; Indhuon could not have dared come here save for the summons of the Shivan-Jalar's daughter. The sight was as new to Indhuon as it was to Simon, and so the young ensign was able to experience the full wonder of it. Here on the upper level, guards held many-tiered parasols of sheer iridescent reptile skins above the counselors, who strutted and preened yet quailed when the Shivan-Jalar so much as glanced in their general direction.

The only one he dared look at was the girl. And how she stared at him! There was magic there. Yes. They had met once or twice, in the cafeteria at the telepathy training summer camp, but she of course had been in the upper-caste food line, dining on delicacies that a prostitute's son could never dream of eating. The thought of those lips biting into the soft shell of a *zerulax* egg—he had put it from his mind. Except once—his arm brushing against hers as the two food lines converged in an X because that year's enrollment was so overcrowded, with the war effort reaching its climax—

And then she'd said, "I heard that."

"I didn't say anything."

"Don't bother denying it. We're in telepathy school. You know you said it."

"It?"

"You know."

And suddenly they had come between them, three enormous cloned nursemaids with fierce expressions, black gowns and wimples, each brandishing a hand-sized laser prod.

"Do *not* address the daughter of the Shivan-Jalar directly, lower-caste scum!" one said.

"I wasn't—"

"Heresy of deed," said the other, "is punishable by a year's cryogenic suspension!'

"Heresy of *thought*," cried the third, "is entirely up to the pleasure of the Mindprober General."

Since then, he had thought of her night and day. He never expected he would be up here, on the shivantic parapet, gazing right into her eyes. She put a finger to her lips. Then, her father still preaching the finer points of theology to his counselors, she slipped away and came up close to him. Immediately, there were nursemaids, but she dismissed them with a flick of the wrist.

"Come for a walk with me," said the most powerful teenaged girl on the entire planet, "and we'll talk. I've been following your dragonboat races since the summer camp ended. I watched the tel-vid of the citywide competition last week. I was thrilled. You know I went to the dock just to see if I could catch a glimpse of you?"

"I thought you wanted to see my little brother—he's the 'great hope,' after all," Indhuon said, unable to keep the envy completely out of his voice.

"Oh, don't think of him that way," she said. There she went, reading his mind again. "Soon he'll be a shining symbol of Tanith's glorious destiny, whereas you and I will—oh! Do you want to kiss me?"

"In front of all these—"

She smiled. "These parapets are more labyrinthine than you think. For instance—"

She took him by the hand. The cloned nursemaids gasped, but did not dare approach. She led him to an area behind her father's throne; it was shaded by a *petrobanyan* tree with spreading branches that took root in the floor, so that the tree was like a many-chambered cave. Crystalline flowers sprouted from crevices and crannies, in eye-popping hues of cerulean, crimson, and fiery yellow. She tugged at his elbow; they ducked behind a wide column of living rock, veined with amethyst and citrine, and despite the massed heat of twin suns, this was a cool place, and she held him tight against the stone; she was warm and the stone was ice-cold against his back, and he himself was all hot and cold at once, and when her lips touched his it was a sensation almost akin to an electric shock; but he didn't mind.

The outpouring of emotion brought Simon to the surface for a moment and he found himself, inside the shared body, passionately kissing Kio in her shared body.

Simon's voice whispered from his mind to Kio's.

This is wrong. You don't want me. Or if you knew me, really knew me, you wouldn't want me.

He could sense her smiling, somewhere in the back of his head—a tickling feeling, almost.

Five thousand years in the past, the ill-fated young ones kissed again. Did they somehow know their days, their hours were numbered? Was that what charged them with such powerful emotion? Or was it just the primal need that propelled all humanoid species toward something called love?

He didn't have time to worry about it, because suddenly the three nursemaid clones came charging into the sanctum.

"You are commanded to the edge of the parapet!" they said in eerie unison. "The race is about to begin!"

The race—from the second to the sixth parapet—was an annual tradition, but each year the victor became the *thanopstru* only symbolically; today it was different. Today, as the climax to the launching of the armada to destroy Thanet once and for all, the *thanopstru* would be sent away for real. It would be the first time in history. And, it was hoped by all, the last.

As Artas lined up with the other competitors, the chanting of the crowd crescendoed. There were hate slogans for the Thanetians, spontaneously it seemed, but in reality whipped up by the city's crack corps of hate police.

They were there for him, those thousands, rooting for him, shouting for him. His mother would be raised up from her lowly station to become anything she chose, perhaps even the tertiary consort of Hal-Therion himself.

On this second parapet, the wind was whipping up his shoulder-length purple-blue hair.

If he won the race, the hair would be shorn.

It was, his mother told him once, his father's hair.

They were calling the names now, using the full formula of given name, matronymic, and clan name: "Beridon siv-Klastru sar-Toth. Anim siren-Taku es-Navik." As the announcer read each name the contestant stepped forward. Each was dressed in the best finery his family could provide. Anim had a cloak of woven chlorquetzal feathers and a headband of ravenlizard pelts; on her wrists were glittering wires of iridium. Beridon wore a tunic of shimmer-fire chased with titanium filigree, and a coronet of rare Northern rushes woven on a loom of ice. And so on and so on, until they reached the tenth name, which was his own: *Artas siv-Taruna es-Sarion.*

And he stepped forth. He was a little self-conscious about his garb; his mother could ill afford the sartorial extravagance of the others, and he wore little but a kilt of crushed paper and a neckpiece of ancient burial jades that had been in his family since an ancestor from the Thieves' Union had stolen it from a Mnemo-Thanasium. It did not matter. When he stepped forward, the crowd broke into a prolongued cheer.

For me! thought Artas.

The footrace was an ancient tradition, its origins so hoary that even the Panvivlion could not describe them. It had been a way to select priests, even kings; in ancient times, a boy could rise to an exalted caste as a result of the footrace.

These days, the traditional run up the Mountain of the Gods was replicated between the second and fifth parapet of the sacred citadel. Four massive ramps, each one replicating every treacherous gully, every outcrop, of the actual mountain, were linked together and led to the Shivantine Stairway, the steps that brought the runner to the very foot of Hal-Therion's throne. The four great streams that were the sources of life's elements were replicated in rivulets of quicksilver, liquid nitrogen, brine, and sulphuric acid. There were other obstacles, too: predators and fearsome beasts, strange twists and turns in the pathway. And from hidden sound devices in the artificial trees, there was the sound of the crowd, whose pleasure or displeasure could spur you on to disaster or victory.

At the sound of a whistle, the runners exchanged their ceremonial garments for the tunic of firestuff and the three sacred objects they would need to reach their goal. Artas held the baton of victory in his right hand; he would win by being the first to touch it to the entrance of the *thanopstru* shell. He placed the hoverboard on the ground; reacting to his unspoken commands, its sensors would carry him past all the obstacles. And around his neck he placed the amulet of his caste, lovingly forged for him at the caste elders' behest, to bring him luck.

He murmured a prayer to the god of celerity, and then he mounted the hoverboard. The other contestants were ready, too. The boards vibrated a little, let out a tinkling sound as they lifted off the stone terrace.

And then they were off!

Easy, easy, he told the board with his mind. *Slow and steady.*

The boards were shooting ahead, angled upward against the contour of the artificial mountain.

He skirted the first rivulet, the quicksilver. The suns' light was dazzling against the liquid metal. This was not a dangerous river if one did not accidentally swallow the toxic mercury, but the liquid nitrogen and the acid flumes could kill. He kept to one side of the stream, carefully rounding a massive dendron tree. He had this part memorized. The first kid had gone whizzing uphill and had dashed himself against bare rock. Artas could not bear to look. *Steady,* he told himself, *steady.*

Artas was nowhere near the head of the line. The front runner was Beridon, whom some considered the favorite, though Artas knew that in the betting parlors of the city she held a slight edge. His brother had bet some money on Beridon—"so as not to jinx you," he had told him with a smile.

Beridon was moving by leaps and bounds. She was even managing a few virtuoso turns, somersaulting onto the board, kicking her leg behind in a graceful arabesque—all hoverboard show tricks that did not really belong in a race for the future of the world. Grimly, Artas guided his board through the obstacle course. He knew she was just doing those tricks in order to confuse the others, to drive them to despair.

Steady! he told the board. *Steady.* His mind was focused now. Yes! Here, the hanging rock. There, the ledge with the treacherous tree. Another runner was trying to go around the tree and kept getting caught in its branches, with their heat-seeking, flesh-eating flowers waiting to snap off a child's hand or foot. There, the kid was loose now, but the board was spinning out of control—

Up! he screamed with his mind, sending the board on a steep curve to avoid the killing tree. *Perfect!* He swerved now, passing someone on the left. Higher up were the ravines of amethyst.

The crowd's roar was dull, distant.

He didn't listen to it. It was like the whisper of the

wind. Artas concentrated as he rounded another rock formation. A tunnel now. He had it memorized, a zigzag path, two lefts, two rights, left, right, right, now suddenly a corkscrew, a gravity well wrenching his gut as he let the board up and around in a corkscrew, the tips of his toes clinging by sheer inertia. Then he was through. The next parapet was easier in a way. The obstacles were all in the mind. Monsters, creatures of darkness. A shadowbeast lurching from a cave. Fangs. Bloodshot eyes. *You're not real,* he thought. *Concentrate. Concentrate.* Smashed right through the illusion. Gore and entrails exploded around him but when he concentrated once more they had dissolved into thin air and—

I'm pulling ahead!

Right in front of him, weaving through a forest of twenty-meter demon statues, some twins he had seen in the training camp, riding in tandem. They were doing figure eights around each other in the air. Each loop was greeted by whoops from the crowd below. *Ignore them!* he told himself. And buzzed right over the twins' heads, did a quick spin, caromed along an acid firewall—and then, breaking over a chasm where he could see straight down onto the sea of people far below, he heard the cheering—and his name—chanted, over and over, like a litany: *Ar-TAS, Ar-TAS, Ar-TAS.*

A whirlwind was chasing them now, spewing from a rock cleft, laced with hallucinogenic gases that plucked dark images from the unconscious. The whirlwind swept uphill, catching the twins in its path. Artas could hear them screaming.

The wind was after him now, tendrils of noxious fumes reaching out toward him, the ends of the tendrils shaped like giant claws. He dodged, darted, slammed the board against a mirror-flat basalt wall to switch gravities and soared up high over the whirlwind, catching a faint whiff, trying to block the nightmare figures that immediately flooded his mind—

The final parapet of the race was just above his head—there were massive metal rivets on its underside that bolted it to the artificial mountainside. The last part was all that remained of the ancient race— no hoverboards now, no hallucinogenic gases, just an uphill track, a straight run toward the throne of the Shivan-Jalar.

A series of rope ladders hung over the edge of the parapet. Anim es-Navik had already jettisoned his hoverboard, pushing against its flexible surface to perform a death-defying catapult onto the first rung of the nearest ladder. Below, he could see that four of the contestants were still in the running.

The whirlwind still had the twins; they were spinning around inside it, and the wind was amplifying their shrieks, broadcasting them to the distant crowd. Artas wondered how they could still be alive. There was so much terror in that wind.

Suddenly the twins had outfoxed the whirlwind, broken free, and now, both riding a single hoverboard, were arrowing upward toward the base of the final parapet. Artas had to make the leap too now.

Good-bye, he thought at the hoverboard. The board steadied itself. He flexed his ankles three times, feeling the spring in it. In front of him, the sheer face of the artificial mountain. Above, the rope ladders dangling from the side of the next parapet. Beneath, the crowd, crawling around like hive ants. He stretched out his hand, gauging the swing of the rope ladder. The wind roared.

Artas leaped.

And in that moment, the whirlwind caught him by his toe and spun him around. Suddenly his head filled with images—the deviving chamber—he knew the death must come, had been told about the ritual blows, the insertion of the wireprobes into the skull, the toxins seeping into the blood—nothing to fear. He had always known it must be this way.

The fumes were spiraling around him now. He could see other images. Himself, millennia hence, trapped, drowning, unable to claw free from a coffin of a prison—monsters now, bogeymen, night-creatures, all gazing at him through the glass—being speechless, unable to feel, touch, taste the world except through sensory organs of metal and pseudo-flesh and—

Fire now, racing through the alleys on an unknown city. A woman's hair flaming. A girl on fire, trying to quench herself in a lake that was beginning to boil—people racing through the streets—a man's face melting—piles of charred flesh—a crowd of hollow-eyed children pointing at the sky, chanting *Artas, Artas, Artas*—but not in admiration. No. In *hate*.

No! he cried out in his mind.

You're going to kill a whole planet, a voice whispered.

No! he screamed.

And then, out of nowhere, it seemed that a hand reached out for him. Grabbed his wrist. Yanked him out of the miasma of nightmare. Thrust him against the lowest rung of the rope ladder. The wind was whipping his face, lashing his hair against his cheeks. He squeezed his eyes tight shut, still tormented by the terror. Whose hand was it? *You!* he thought. *The one I saw this morning! What are you to me?*

Artas, the voice whispered. *It's me, Adam Halliday—the kid from the future.*

Artas hung on to the ladder. It was swinging in the wind. With a supreme effort, he heaved his body up to the next rung—and the next—

Stay with me, he told the inner voice. *Please—I need someone—*

I can't help but stay with you, said Adam. *I'm stuck inside your mind.*

Artas squeezed his eyes tight shut. Thought of all the training exercises, all the times on a rope ladder such as this with only a few meters between him and the training floor—not like this, swinging in a roaring wind, kilometers above ground level. He thought of his mother.

And then there was another image in his mind. A beautiful woman from another world. A woman who could reach into the very depths of his being.

The vision flickered and was gone. Then there came the voice of the child.

The inner voice said, *I can't get out of your mind.*

Artas whispered, *Stay.*

Everything was blurry. There was no crowd, no competition. Only the rough rope against his sore palms, shredding skin now. He pulled himself up. In his mind he saw the angel, the boy from the future, whatever he was—floating against the starstream, arms stretched out toward him, drawing him up out of hell—in an ocean of stars—his hands strangely webless, alien—his hair glittering against the streaking starlight—pulling him, up, up, up—and—

There was the final run now, a dash of a few hundred meters, all up a steep smooth slope toward the throne of the Shivan-Jalar. Only a few in the race—three or four at best. He couldn't really see them because of the sweat pouring down his face, spurting into his eyes. His eyes smarted, his lips were stung by the briny taste—and here the wind was fierce, unrelenting.

He ran.

He was dimly aware of the others. They too were like him, all the hopes and dreams of their families riding on this one dash toward glory. They too were full of hatred for the Thanetians. They too were pumped up with slogans and pep talks from trainers and religious leaders. They too had drunk themselves silly on potions designed for strength, agility, and indifference to pain—potions that also led to hallucinations and secret terrors. They too were afraid.

Perhaps, they too had received visitations from angels—they too believed themselves to be the chosen one. But only one angel could be a true angel. For angels do not lie.

Look! There were the twins. They were whooping as they ran, but Artas was faster. He swept by them. And now there was someone else, just ahead. He didn't remember seeing that kid before. Someone running in a cloud of luminescence. Someone haloed in rainbow light. *I've got to catch up to him! I've got to!* he thought. He was aware of pain, fiery pain in his ankles and thighs, but he couldn't stop. There was that one person left to beat, to overtake.

He ran.

Catching up now—catching up—

He could see the stranger's face—his own face.

Then, for a split second, he was in a glass cage, and a dozen faces in one-piece jumpsuits were staring at him with pained, compassionate eyes. Then the vision faded.

He wasn't even thinking of winning anymore. All he was thinking of was running. Not here, not uphill in the burning suns' light, but in the tall purple grass beside the ocean—not for an audience of millions but for himself alone—he ran.

I am a comet.

Slicing through the emptiness. The lonely gray spaces between the stars. *I am a comet.*

He ran.

At the edge of time and space, the angel stood with outstretched arms, a mirror image of himself.

Artas, the angel said.

Are you my mother?

No.

But she's the reason I'm running—she's the reason I'm giving up my life—so she can be *someone—so her caste won't stop her from becoming anything she chooses.*

Oh, Artas, no, I'm not your mother—but—

Someone like his mother, though, only with dark, haunting eyes and hair that fell in dusky ringlets—a strange half-smile—a woman he'd never seen before and yet who somehow *knew* him, understood his innermost thoughts.

You must *be an angel!* he thought.

He ran toward the angel, ran toward the warm embrace of love and light, but suddenly.

Cold! Bitter, unforgiving emptiness! And rage, terrible rage, rage directed inward at himself, ripping himself apart, and—

The eyes of the Shivan-Jalar.

They seemed to penetrate his very soul.

He closed his eyes. *I'm dying,* he thought. And fell prostrate at the feet of the high throne.

Chapter Nineteen

Instrument of Fate

WITHIN THE LIMBO of the *dailong*'s simulation matrix, minds past and future revolved and intertwined with Data's consciousness. Artas's elation blended with Adam's certain knowledge of the comet's future. His mother's pride and sorrow melded with Counselor Troi's empathy and torrent of child-rage that engulfed her.

As Artas looked up, the godlike countenance of the Shivan-Jalar was made brilliant by the confluence of the two suns' radiance. He raised his arm; his hand held an orb of power, encrusted with precious gems, and containing a rare liquid, the ambrosia of the gods, which was refined *peftifesht*, a thousand times stronger than the brew served in the taverns of the prostitutes' quarter.

"Artas," said the Shivan-Jalar, his voice reverberant and strangely calm above the sea of cheering far below. "You have achieved what no other child has ever achieved in our five-thousand-year-old history. For though there is a footrace every year, and a *thanopstru* is selected each season to rides in honor at the head of the parade of honor along the sacred Boulevard of Righteous Hatred—you are actually going for a ride in the great comet. May the spirits of the five thousand who went ahead of you be always present to guide you in your holy mission."

Artas remained prostrate in front of the great throne. Except for that one moment, when he had stared right into the face of the most high, he had kept his eyes downcast, as was proper in the presence of the one who spoke in the place of all the gods.

"Come closer, boy," said the Shivan-Jalar. "Come—sit here. At the foot of the throne. I'm going to have a talk with you—and no one else shall hear what we say to one another." He clapped his hands. Miraculously, the entire council retreated into the background. Guards came forward and clamped a wall of metal shields around the throne.

"You will be the *thanopstru*. Do you know what that means? Do you truly, truly know, child?"

"It means I will rain fire on our enemies, and they will perish."

"What do you know about Thanet?"

"They are our enemies. We hate them."

"And why, my son, why?"

"It has always been so."

"But why has it always been so, my son?"

"Because we hate the Thanetians. It's our whole reason for being. The gods created us to hate each other—and to try to destroy one another. My teacher said the whole universe is about duality. I don't know what that means, but I think it's that we need to balance them against us."

The Shivan-Jalar nodded slowly. "In a few short hours you will undergo a metamorphosis that many have theorized about, but no one has truly experienced. The fact is, Artas, that no one knows what it will be like—only you will know, and no one alive today will be alive when you arrive to find out the things you will know."

"Why not, Holy Father?"

"Because, my son, we cannot know for certain if we have yet conquered the speed of light. We have reached an accommodation with it, certainly; our drones, carrying weapons of mass destruction, will travel by a new superluminal drive, and be delivered to our enemies almost instantly. But a *thanopstru* needs the intelligence of a living brain to power it, and there is a warping that occurs at the moment when we cross the speed of light, something modern science has been unable to overcome—a flattening effect combined with an increase in mass almost to the level of infinity for one minuscule microsecond, enough to destroy a living thing. The transwarp drive in the *thanopstru* is an experimental thing; it has never been tested. There are three possibilities. If the drive functions perfectly, you will arrive in the Klastravo system at the same time as the drones of lesser destructive power, and Thanet will be no more—this time without the possibility of recovery, for its very atmosphere will have been stripped away. Secondly, it may function well enough, but your consciousness may be destroyed on the way, so that there will be no one with the finely tuned reflexes and psychic control of the *thanopstru*'s quasi-neural functions; if so, the destruction wreaked by the *thanopstru* will be random at best, and the comet may even explode harmlessly in space, or fall into Klastravo and be pulverized. The third possibility is the strangest one of all to contemplate. What if the superluminal drive malfunctions? What if you are forced to travel at sublight speed, a five-thousand-year journey, toward a planet only partially destroyed by the drones?

"Think of the irony of such a scenario! The world that you reach will already have been devastated by the drones, but you will destroy all that remains of it—any straggling remnants of humanity, any attempts by the Thanetians to regain the status of a civilized world. Your task, Artas, will have been the total annihilation of people five thousand years in the future, who may have no awareness whatsoever of this war, this ancient hatred—or whose knowledge of it may be only in the form of myth. Do you understand this? Could you contemplate such a possibility and not self-destruct in shame and horror?"

"I don't need to understand this, Holy Father," Artas said. "I am an instrument of fate. I will be the *thanopstru.*"

"Yes, my son, you will. And thus it is that you must understand your destiny completely. We and the Thanetians are brothers, as the dark is brother to the light, and the day to the night. For eon upon eon this sacred war has been going on. You learned in school that this is the war that keeps the universe in balance, that it is as much a law of nature as gravity and the speed of light. You have learned about the five-thousand-year cycle and how it renews the cosmos. But the truth is far less clear-cut than that. The origins of the war are shrouded in mystery. One of us colonized the other; in my communication with the computers of past epochs, I have never managed to discover who came first. Some say the war began over a woman; some over an assassination. The five-thousand-year cycle exists because that is the time it takes to travel between our worlds—unless, somehow, the secret of faster-than-light travel ever gets solved completely, which, perhaps, has happened this time. Every five thousand years we crawl up from the slime, every five thousand years it seems that we get to the brink of awesome new discoveries about space travel—and then we launch our weapons.

"Perhaps, one day, there will be complete annihilation, and the cycle will end. Or perhaps the secret of the warp will come sooner in one cycle, and we will actually speak to our enemies face-to-face, and somehow it will end. Or perhaps there will be a time when a new civilization is born out of the conscious-ness of the *dailong* that has no memory of the war at all, just vague legends. And yet somehow the war will go on, and the innocent will perish.

"You cannot know what world it is you will de-stroy. You cannot know whether they will hate us, or even know who you are. Fate, that is all you must be. And you must accept that.

"And before you accept godhead, you must com-prehend it. You are blind fate, my child, you are the instrument of retribution upon the innocent as well as the guilty."

Artas could not truly understand what the Shivan-Jalar was saying. But he realized he might have five thousand years in which to contemplate its meaning. If he read the Shivan-Jalar's meaning at all rightly, the Holy Father was telling him that the design of the *thanosptru* was flawed; that there was only a slim chance that it would all work as planned. The third possibility was the most likely—

Five thousand was an incomprehensible number to the boy; it was, after all, as long as the entire span of recorded history.

But Artas was full of pride, a pride that was also a little like pain. And then came the goblet of ambrosia, poured out of the orb; the wine had been fermenting within the orb for five millennia, and now it was time to drink. First came the ritual strangulation for four small werreti-beasts, and their blood was added to the goblet. Then the incantation to the seven war gods was uttered.

"Take this cup," said the Shivan-Jalar. "And with the first draft, cast off your identity. Forget Tanith. Forget boyhood. Forget this beautiful world, forget the ones you love. Forget even the taste of this ambrosia. Forget all tastes, all sights, smells, sounds; where you are going is only the cold and the emptiness. Forget, Artas."

"I forget," said Artas.

And he drank deep.

"Until Thanet is destroyed, you shall never sleep."

"I shall never sleep." He took another draught of the bitter *peftifesht*.

"You shall not sleep through the warping of space-time, not sleep until the moment comes when you shall set the machineries of death in motion."

"I shall not sleep."

"You shall not sleep even should the hyperdrive fail, and you be forced to fly the lonely journey in real time."

"No, I shall not sleep, for I am the *thanopstru*."

"The force that shall fuel you will be cold hatred, and hatred shall run in your veins instead of blood, and hatred will animate your every thought."

"I shall hate." He drank again.

"You are the emissary of fate."

"I am fate itself." He drank.

A strange coldness seeped into his limbs. Two guards lifted him up by his arms—a slip of a child he was, frail and impassive as the power of the forti-fied *peftifesht* took hold of him.

"Are you forgetting?" the Shivan-Jalar said softly.

"I am forgetting," said Artas, his voice settling into a strange monotone.

"Do you have any last wishes?" said the Shivan-Jalar. "Soon you will speak no more."

"My mother," he said. "Couldn't she—couldn't she be happy?"

The Holy Father clapped his hands. Almost instantly, they brought his mother to him, carrying her on a perfumed bier; though she wore the insignia of the prostitutes' caste, she was appareled in such luxury she could have been a queen, or a demigoddess.

"Taruna es-Sarion," the guard announced.

"Let this be the last time you are called by that name," said the Shivan-Jalar, raising his orb high. "For now you shall be called Taruna Batar Thanopstratis, the Mother of the Star of Death. Your image shall be placed at the entranceway to every Mnemo-Thanasium and High Temple in the world. And with this ritual deathblow"—he gave a command, and a guard rushed toward her with a scimitar, and pretended to decapitate her—"I end your former life, and bring you to a rebirth as a member of the high caste of Errolam."

The people around them gasped. Errolam was one of the highest of all castes, reserved only for the concubines of the highest religious authorities. Artas could see, through the veil of *peftifesht*-induced confusion, that his mother was in a transport of emotion. Perhaps she was to be the consort of the Shivan-Jalar himself! Vaguely, he could sense the excitement of all around; but the *peftifesht* was dulling his mind—he was already withdrawing from the world of the senses.

"Taruna s'Errolam," said the Shivan-Jalar. "Are you content?"

"Yes, my lord," she said as she prostrated herself from her position on the bier.

"And your son," said the Shivan-Jalar, "shall be my daughter's consort, for I see they are already much taken with each other."

"You do my family prime honor," said his mother, and placed her folded palms to her lips in a gesture of gratitude.

"Then kiss your child farewell."

Taruna descended from the litter. She took her child in her arms. Artas wanted to embrace her warmly, wanted to crush her to him, show her how much he loved her, how he had done this for her, not for any personal glory—but the drug was working fast now, and consciousness was becoming murkier moment by moment.

"My son," she said softly.

Mother! he cried out in his mind, but she could not hear him.

But five thousand years thence, another woman did hear. A woman not his mother, but who had felt his mother's feelings—her elation, her bereavement.

Who are you? he cried out in his mind.

A single word, incomprehensible, reverberated in his head: *Troi, Troi, Troi.*

And the other woman called to him through the chaos of space-time: *Artas, Artas, do not weep.*

Chapter Twenty

Devivement

"THIS IS APPALLING," Deanna Troi cried, and Picard, watching the spectacle unfold on multiple screens on the bridge of the *Enterprise,* could not have agreed more.

Picard said, "Counselor, perhaps you should withdraw."

"No," she said. "Captain, I have to experience this until the very end. I can't analyze this situation with only half the information."

"Dr. Crusher?" Picard said.

"It's taking its toll," said Beverly. "But her vital signs are still—viable."

Picard said, "Counselor, I'll leave this to your own judgment. I know that you will pull out of this cybernetic melding if you sense too much danger to yourself."

But Deanna did not respond; she had already re-submerged herself in the ancient story.

There were steps to ascend; hundreds of steps, and hundreds of high officials in their robes of state. The smaller sun had crossed the face of the larger; the heat was almost unbearable. Artas, now clothed only in the translucent Cloak of the Invincible, was being carried up the steps by eight guards on a boy-sized golden shield. He lay as though dead.

Indhuon, walking beside him, knew that his brother was not yet dead. There was still some human consciousness left in him, but soon that would be gone as his mind was joined to the greater consciousness of the *thanopstru*. Next to him was Ariela. He could scarcely believe he had gone from his humble origins to the consort-elect of the Shivan-Jalar's daughter, but Artas's supreme sacrifice was already bringing his family some of the greatest rewards one could achieve in this world.

Above them, the shell of the *thanopstru* glittered against the face of the double sun, almost blinding; on the first step beneath it, the devivement cylinder, in which Artas would go to immortality. Once he entered the cylinder, the boy would be considered a god.

And he would be brother to a god—and one of the most sought-after men on the planet.

Indhuon watched as a doorway opened in the cylinder. The honor guards lifted the shield up, and then the four nearest the cylinder knelt down so that his brother could be slid into the tiny cavity inside. Within, Indhuon knew, coma-inducing gases seethed. Once his brother was completely sedated, tendrils of silicon-based pseudolife would begin to invade his body, slithering up into his brain, sharing his identity, stealing his soul and reprogramming it with nothing but the desire to kill.

Now, according to the ritual formula, the relatives of the god would have to turn their backs on the boy, one by one. There were only two relatives present, of course; Indhuon knew that a man who gives a prostitute a child would never acknowledge such a thing, and so there was only his mother and himself, no band of weeping, proud relatives.

He gripped Ariela's hand, and broke away to stand beside the shield. His mother was there too. She had descended from her litter, and was standing over Artas's face, resolutely holding back her tears. Her new robes of the caste of Errolam shimmered in the suns. A coronet of light swathed her luxuriant hair. *My mother is truly beautiful,* Indhuon thought. It was the streak of sadness in her, accentuating the darkness around her eyes, the hint of worry at the edges of her lips, that made her all the more beautiful.

The turning of the back ceremony was to happen in order of age; therefore, Indhuon would be the last creature of flesh and blood to lay eyes on his brother's face. After that, the cylinder would be closed, as a coffin was closed before being consigned to the Mnemo-Thanasium. The former Artas would be dead and the god would be born.

How must his mother be feeling? Indhuon thought. *His mother—my mother.*

Deanna could hear Taruna's thoughts, as clearly as if they were speaking face-to-face. She was thinking *Yes, yes, I will be consort to a demigod now, it's what I've always wished. I'll try to forget the one I hugged, the one I sang to sleep—I'll try to forget but I know I'm going to be haunted by it, oh gods, I remember the blast of blinding pain when I knew he was emerging from me, he was such a difficult birth, I remember holding him and he wouldn't even cry, wouldn't even make a sound, as if he already knew he wasn't going to stay with me very long, as if to say Mother, Mother, don't be too close to me—how I love you, my Artashki, my angel, my pride.*

Though Deanna's body was still in the heart of the comet, connected through Data and the *dailong*'s monstrous network of links to this distant events, her mind was right there in the ancient world; she could see the vibrant colors of the city, double-brilliant and double-shadowed by the dance of its twin suns, she could see, through Taruna's eyes, the boy, his hands folded across his chest like a Pharaoh about to be mummified; his eyes were still open, unblinking; they were windows into a yawning emptiness.

* * *

And Taruna turned away from her son's face, and now it was the brother's turn. Indhuon stroked his brother's face; already it seemed to have grown cold.

"Good-bye, little brother," he said.

The cylinder closed.

A primitive device of metal wires and pulleys hoisted it upright.

In front of them, there was the *thanopstru:* a metallic sphere, its surface artificially pitted to resemble a natural object.

Looking at the alien past through Indhuon's eyes, Simon Tarses was interested in the workings of the *thanopstru.* As it rose up, a crystalline humming permeated the air, and from far below a collective murmur from the crowd swelled like a gathering ocean storm. There was nothing in this technology that appeared to resemble any device of the Federation. Whatever this was, it was an independent discovery.

I wish I knew more, Simon thought.

And then he heard, echoing through the conduit of Data's mind, the response—*So do I.*

Simon looked through Indhuon's eyes and saw Ariela, and behind Ariela's eyes he knew that the consciousness of Kio was present—and that Kio and Ariela shared a genetic connection that spanned many five-thousand-year cycles. That was the reason, no doubt, for the rigid caste system defined in the Panvivlion; it kept the families intact from cycle to cycle no matter who was lost.

I wish I could kiss you, Simon thought.

But you can! came Kio's thoughts.

And suddenly he realized it was true, for the diplomatic necessities that divided Simon and Kio did not affect Indhuon and Ariela. Quite the opposite; everything and everyone smiled upon the union of the two Tanithians.

Before he could finish the thought, it was happening. Indhuon and Ariela were clinging to each other. And the Shivan-Jalar, immersed in his recitation from the Panvivlion, didn't move to stop them. They kissed, and thus it was that Simon and Kio also kissed, each finding the taste of alien lips strangely intoxicating.

How strange it is, Simon thought. *For years I've been haunted by an event that made me feel an outcast among people who were supposed to accept me. Now, among aliens, in an alien body, I feel a sense of belonging. There is something about this young woman that reaches only me. A secret message that has been written for me alone. That has waited for me on the other side of the galaxy, that would have gone unsaid if this one-in-a-trillion confluence of chance events had not occurred.* It was almost enough to make him buy the Thanetian concept of total predestination.

The *thanopstru* was now halfway up the sky, and the suns were setting. The pits and blemishes were invisible now. Artas was a sphere of light, glittering, brilliant, a new star burning blue-white against the deepening sky.

Now, traditionally, would follow a night of celebration, a night for the downing of *peftifesht* and the chewing of *xakuna* leaves. There would be merriment and laughter and Artas would be toasted in a million households. Sending death to Thanet was the supreme joy.

It was then that Indhuon saw the strange lights in the sky.

He could hear curious murmurings around him. The Shivan-Jalar's council was pointing, staring. The crowd, far below, stirred.

There were thousands of them, points of light that wove in and out of each other, multicolored, dancing, darting—

"Thanet!" the Shivan-Jalar exclaimed.

Simon, with his historical vantage point, knew right away what was happening. Thanet must be attacking. The five-thousand-year cycle was a thing of eerie precision. Who knew how many cycles had passed, how many times this self-destructive pattern had been played out?

His reaction must have been severe, because it seemed to have bled through into Indhuon's consciousness, and now Indhuon was blurting out: "They're attacking us—the Thanetians are attacking us *again!*"

"Again?" Indhuon noticed the Shivan-Jalar looking at him strangely, as, overhead, more lights speckled the darkling sky.

Indhuon gripped Ariela's hand. The Shivan-Jalar had actually descended from his high seat. He was within arms' length of Indhuon, and the young man knew that to touch the Shivan-Jalar was sacrilege—yet now it seemed no longer to matter. For the Shivan-Jalar was touching *him*—stroking Indhuon's cheek, squeezing his arm, and Indhuon could see tears now, and he could only half-understand why this man, the holiest personage on the planet, would weep, would want to embrace him.

"I thought," said the master of the world, "that I alone was afflicted by visions of previous epochs—that I alone was able to penetrate the veil of darkness that separates us from the world of five thousand years ago."

"Holy Father," Indhuon said, as the first wave of deathstars exploded silently high above the atmosphere, flower-bursts of radiation—too far away yet to harm anyone. These were the premature blasts, weapons that had blown up too far up to destroy—a light show to augur the end. "I've only just begun to hear some inner voice—only now, only today. The voice identifies himself with a strange name: *Simon Tarses*. It is not a language I have ever heard—a language he refers to as *Fe-de-re-shan*."

"Then the scripture is fulfilled," the Shivan-Jalar said softly. "The words in the Panvivlion are: *When dusk falls on the world, the blind shall see, and the seeing shall see beyond; the deaf shall hear, and the hearing shall hear voices from the past and the future.* I have claimed to hear voices, because my high office requires it; often what I said was an echo of an echo, a distorted quote plucked from an ancient text.

But suddenly, yesterday, there was a voice in my head too, one that identified himself as Bo-bha-lee-dei. He is a sage from the future, full of amazing wisdom, and when I see through his eyes I see wonders I have never imaged before. It is because of him that today I addressed my privy council and actually had the courage to make plain the doubts that war within me, doubts that will soon be stilled by the greatest silence man can know. What do *your* voices say?"

"Holy Father," Indhuon said, "they say that we are all going to die—and that our planet will be laid waste, forever this time." And Indhuon marveled, because he who was most high was sharing his secret thoughts with a mere youth, even though that youth was brother to a god. "The creature called Simon Tarses speaks to me from five thousand years in the future—and he seems to know my brother by name—"

"Which means that the race to build the perfect *thanopstru* is lost," said the Holy Father, "and Tanith will not survive. They did it first. And ours will fail. Our hyperdrive is an illusion. Our scientists have created—*nothing!* Our entire civilization has had no meaning at all!"

"No, my lord!" cried Indhuon.

And then Ariela spoke. "How can you say that, Father? You know that time levels all accomplishments. It says so in the Panvivlion. We're lucky to have seen what we've seen. I'm lucky because even though we'll be dead in a few minutes, I'm in love, and my last kiss is going to be illuminated by the grandest fireworks display of all time, and—" She was racked with sobs, and Indhuon held her tight, feeling her slight frame thrust hard against him. Was this really love? There would be no more chances to find out. And so they kissed again, in public, forgetting all shame, and Ariela's father said nothing.

The god-king of Tanith only blinked back his tears.

Far below, the mob was restless, but they did not yet realize the end was imminent; doubtless they thought the display in the sky was just the celebratory fireworks. Indeed, he could hear cheering and chanting of slogans—perhaps he was only imagining the undercurrent of unease.

"They will know soon enough," said the Holy Father. "Another two or three attack waves, and death will begin to rain down." He motioned to the guards. The entire conversation had taken place within a small perimeter; the council, apprehensive, was not privy to it. They saw only a young man receiving unheard-of favor from the highest in the land, and Indhuon could see them chattering among themselves, still, even now, plotting for advancement, wondering who would next rise and fall in the Shivan-Jalar's favor.

The Shivan-Jalar placed his hands on the heads of his daughter and Indhuon. Ariela knelt down, and Indhuon, sensing a moment of great solemnity, went down on his knees beside her.

"When you arise," said the Shivan-Jalar, "you shall be one flesh, and joint heirs to all that is mine;

I declare that you are wed now, the last lovers of the world, the last beautiful thing we can produce to show that we, the Tanithian peoples, once possessed a noble civilization in a watery world in a remote arm of the great galaxy. Rise, my son and daughter. Rise and inherit what's left of the world."

And from deep inside himself, Indhuon heard the voice of the creature named Simon Tarses whisper.

"Mother."

He looked up. An acrid scent was seeping through the atmosphere. He knew that it was poison. Above, the deathstars were shooting back and forth, their trails spiraling, corkscrewing, weaving intricate patterns of destruction. He gazed at the parapets below him. The artificial mountain his brother had climbed to godhood was already aflame. Rivers of acid had become rivers of lethal fumes. Fire was running down the slopes. Men and women were ablaze. He could not hear the screaming clearly through the shield of force. It was all enacted in miniature. For a few moments, Indhuon had the perspective of a god.

And he thought of his brother.

For five thousand years, he would never sleep.

Artas! she cried out in her mind—

Her last thought was of her child in her arms—rocking him to sleep—humming an ancient lullaby—

And the sky was burning.

* * *

Far below, fire ran down the streets—the city was a burning skein—and the two lovers kissed, and through their lips two lovers of the distant future kissed also—for one pair, existence was ending; for the other, life was just beginning—

The *thanopstru* sliced through the world's atmosphere in an instant—and Artas floated in the half-world—his body was metal now, invulnerable—his nerves were of silicon—his eyes saw all around him through hundreds of photosensors on the comet's surface—he hurtled through the emptiness—and Adam, still linked to the *thanopstru*'s consciousness, felt the power of it all, could feel the drunkenness of power and *peftifesht* coursing through his system—

If a lonely boy with extraordinary talents were given the chance to *be* something this important, this potent—Adam felt Artas's rage, too, how it was being chaneled toward this one moment of destruction that must come, inevitably, this moment when a boy would have the annihilating power of godhead.

And yet—

Beneath that rage there was something else too.

The loneliness.

Adam remembered how he'd wandered the corridors of the institute, before his father had sent for him to come to Thanet; he remembered, too, walking the streets of Thanet all by himself, never belonging, always the outsider. He had seen deep into

Artas's soul with even his limited empathic abilities. There was a reason he had been chosen to be linked to Artas. Perhaps it was the influence of Thanet's fate-driven culture that made him think so, but the feeling ran deeper than that.

A thousand kilometers over Tanith—two thousand—only in an instant it seemed. And then Artas saw—and Adam saw through Artas's thousand eyes, the panels on the smooth surface of the artificial comet—

First, the world itself.

An ocean world; blue and white, cloud-wrapped, colors of moonstone and sapphire. The world's six continents set in the ocean like emerald mosaic stones, tiny against the expanse of blue.

Beautiful and doomed.

It was beginning now. The oceanside metropolis set in the largest of the island continents was starting to glow. Artas could see pinpricks of blinding fire. And now the fire was spilling out of the city, running in rivulets across the continent. He knew that each rivulet must be a hundred kilometers wide for him to be able to see it here—a spiderweb of flame now, spreading, spreading—and the atmosphere was changing color, darkening, as a poison began to spread—thousands of shooting stars were falling into the atmosphere, igniting as they hit oxygen— Artas thought of his mother and brother—*I sacrificed everything for them,* he thought—*my death was supposed to make her the most important woman in*

199

the world—a saint, the consort of a god—and now— it's come to nothing—nothing at all—

Except—wouldn't there be survivors? There always had been, if he understood what the Shivan-Jalar had been going on about in Artas's last moments of being human.

His rage grew.

Then, out of nothingness—

From between the twin suns it came—an orb of spinning light with a dozen tails—in moments it had grown from a point to a circle—

The enemy's thanopstru! Artas thought.

He had to disengage the hyperdrive somehow, had to steer himself into a position to stop it! *If I collide with it head on,* he thought. Artas sent commands to the comet's onboard nerve center. He worked the waldoes inside the comet's chambers as easily as if they were his own limbs—he tugged at the new memories he was now connected to, pulling out specs and plans, trying to rig the computer to override its programmed pathway—

"Behold," the Shivan-Jalar whispered. "What a privilege it is to witness the world's ending."

The privy council was gathered around the throne now, each of them prostrate, in awe, making a formal tableau of obeisance to the power of the gods. If any of them felt fear or panic, they had mastered it; the inevitability of death made panic meaningless.

God for a day, Dr. Halliday was thinking, as he

peered at the burning minarets through the eyes of the Shivan-Jalar.

For a moment, a single moment, Ariela was thinking as tendrils of poison began to slither into the holiest of holies. And she kissed her beloved one more time, trying to draw the moment out as best she could, but the poison was already corrupting her breathing, and the tears were beginning to spurt from the acrid fumes.

The last thing Taruna saw, as the tide of deathlight swept across the sky—

Artas, alone, forsaken, in the cold dark emptiness of space, and—

The angel.

"Save my son," she murmured. The heat was unendurable.

The angel stood there, against the burning city, a thousand times the height of a man, the angel with the dark ringlets and haunting eyes, the angel who had called herself Deanna—she stood there with her arms outstretched—

"My son—you will be with him—in that desolate future—you must save him—promise me—*promise me!*" Taruna screamed.

And the angel smiled an enigmatic smile before she dissipated and the fire consumed Taruna.

The comet dodged! And swerved! *I could smash headlong into him,* Artas thought. *But then I would fail in my mission—never to sleep until Thanet is destroyed.* He steered the *thanopstru* back into the path of the enemy. *Perhaps if I come so close that it has to change flight path or be destroyed—*

This was dangerous, so dangerous. The boys of Tanith had a game they played with their hoverboards, facing each other across a bridge, accelerating toward each other, seeing who would lose his nerve first—

Artas did not understand. He knew only that the creature he had seen that morning—when he still lived in the alley of the pleasure women—was still with him. "Give me strength," his mind whispered, "whoever you are, whatever—"

The *thanopstru* was a large-scale weapon, designed to shatter a world—not to battle other star vessels at close quarters. It had a primitive system of shields and a few defensive banks of energy beams that could be deployed, but they drew energy from the experimental hyperdrive.

I can take him out, Artas thought.

With a supreme effort, he wrenched himself off course and set an intersect flight path toward his enemy and—

Lashed out, death beams that seemed to come from a thousand fingers—

He had grazed the enemy! The Thanetian *thanopstru* was spinning out of control. Artas drew more power, pursued—

The Thanetian dodged. Artas darted.

The Thanetian began to tumble toward Tanith's atmosphere and—

Artas spun away.

Was there another lonely boy inside that comet, programmed with implacable hatred?

No time to think of that. Artas reversed course, plunged himself downward toward the gravity well, knowing in his heart that it was too late—

The demon comet was a fireball—soon it would impact on the main continent—and Artas realized in moments he too was going to add to the destruction of his homeworld.

The enemy *thanopstru* was on a collision course with Tanith, and nothing would stop it. It would activate. Everyone would die. Everyone.

It was too late to save them. Only vengeance remained.

Artas reached out with his nerves of silicon, his sinews of steel—reached into the comet's core to pull out every erg of energy from its sputtering warp drive. He dredged up his last remaining strength. The gravity well was drawing him in. He tried to wrest himself away, like a wayward child struggling free from his mother's arms. Tanith was his mother, holding on, calling his name, but Tanith was no more, and only hate remained.

In a moment the warp drive would kick in.

In a moment he would get his revenge.

He was beyond the star system now, and the twin spheres of Tanith's suns were already becoming just two more stars, still the brightest, but no longer dominating the blackness of space.

Engage! he commanded the comet's drive. His silicon nerves locked on, his brain sent the preprogrammed signal that would activate the faster-than-light engines.

But there was nothing.

The Shivan-Jalar had been right. The worst-case scenario was in effect.

He had five thousand years of waking dream ahead of him, five thousand years for hate to fester, to grow, to become unstoppable.

The angel named Adam said, *We'll meet again.*
And faded.

On Tanith, there was light—

Part Four:
The Planet That Waited for Death

The Shivan-Jalar is my protector; I am but a crumb
  that has fallen from his table.
The High Shivantak is as the right hand of the
  Shivan-Jalar; he shall be to me as a god.
They shall lead me toward the fields of light;
They shall squeeze for me the juice of the peftifesht,
And I shall neither hunger nor thirst.
But for them would I have no soul,
But for them would I sing no song.
What to me is the shadow of death?
Death is but a shadow,
And the Shivan-Jalar is the light.

—from the Holy Panvivlion

ONCE AGAIN, PICARD TURNED to Dr. Halliday's field notes. Soon, the Captain would face the High Shivantak himself. He needed all the information he could glean.

CONFIDENTIAL REPORT:

Dr. Robert Halliday's field notes

Let me try to say a few words about the religion of the Thanetians. I have been trying to make sense of it all since getting here.

First, as I've said in previous reports, they believe that everything that has ever happened will happen again, and that everything that is happening now has already happened. I don't know how many members of the board reading these notes are familiar with ancient India, but that's an important old Earth civilization with the same cyclical view of the universe. They also used to have a caste system, but nothing like as intricate as the one here, with the complex dietary laws attendant upon each.

Their concept of godhood is very interesting. Superficially, there seem to be many of them, and they're always invoking various gods when they are annoyed. There's even a god for constipation. And there are statues of the gods everywhere, of course, shrines, little nooks on street corners where one can leave offerings, and so on; that too is like ancient India and such cultures. But when it comes to putting your finger on a god as a supernatural being, the Thanetians become pretty nebulous. They will start to tell you that all the gods are aspects of each other, and when you press them they will say that the High Shivantak is the sole person who can interpret the nature of godhead. And the High Shivantak, so far, isn't talking, although there are times when I think that he appropriates the essence of godhood unto himself.

The High Shivantak, in theory, rules as the regent for the Shivan-Jalar, except that there hasn't been one of those in all of Thanet's recorded history. From time to time, the Shivantak makes pronouncements in the name of the Shivan-Jalar, and many assume he is communicating with that mythical being by way of some kind of psychic projection. Another possibility is that he is simply making it all up in order to appear even more powerful than he actually is.

His position is by no means ceremonial, even though bureaucrats do just about everything on Thanet; his every whim is catered to, and he is the one person on Thanet who is exempt from the heresy laws.

Ah, yes, those heresy laws! Once in a while, their equivalent of the Spanish Inquisition goes on a rampage, and, barbaric as it sounds, they actually *do* burn people at the stake. It's a very sophisticated stake, with all the trappings of higher civilization, but a stake nonetheless. If one says the wrong thing, a heresy trial can be a drawn-out process, and lawyers for such cases belong to a caste that is not allowed to enter public buildings; they must project a hologram into the court to avoid contamination by a heretic's touch. As one can imagine, then, there is a lot of prejudgment involved as soon as the word "heretic" is invoked, and few are acquitted. This witch-hunting orthodoxy is the darkness that underlies the mozaic-like beauty of this planet's culture.

When the High Shivantak leaves his roost, his feet are not permitted to touch the ground. He rides on a palanquin powered by a low-level

antigravity device, with ceremonial guards
before and behind. Half-naked woman with
censers walk in front of the guards to strew
flowers and spread the fragrance of his divinity
around. As one might imagine, it's not
conducive to humility. Indeed, the caste system
itself tends to intensify people's propensity to
lord it over others, and to grovel; there's always
someone to be better than, and worse than, in
this society.

The High Shivantak's day is circumscribed
by ritual. His rising and sleeping are regulated
by astrological calculations; and each evening
he must speak a blessing from the uppermost
story of his palace over the entire city. Some
Thanetians wait outside in the square all
afternoon in order to receive the blessing
personally. It is believed that receiving one
thousand or more such blessings in the course
of a lifetime will cause the supplicant to be
reborn, during the next five-thousand-year
cycle, in a caste one grade higher than his
present caste. Since there seem to be a pretty
much endless number of caste grades, this more
or less ensures a constant presence of a vast
throng outside the palace from early afternoon
onward. There are also those who believe that
the dawn will not come without the blessing
having been given the previous evening.

There are many rumors about the High

Shivantak, some of which are gossipy
speculation of the sort that any high royal is
bound to have said about him: his sexual habits,
his gluttony, and so on.

Far more useful to the Federation is the
belief, held by most people in the capital city,
that the High Shivantak has a habit of "playing
both ends against the middle," and that he
keeps his bureaucrats constantly on their toes
by assigning them to secret missions and
then—deliberately, it is said—forgetting those
missions completely.

In other words, he out-Machiavellis
Machiavelli, if any of you Federation
bureaucrats have any memory of who
Machiavelli was.

Chapter Twenty-One

Asylum

PICARD LOOKED AWAY from Halliday's field notes. There was much fascinating material here, and also much of Halliday's own personality—smug and self-congratulatory at times, but also keenly incisive and knowledgeable. This High Shivantak was clearly a mass of contradictions, and the more that was known about him, the better.

Picard wore full dress uniform, in preparation for an audience with the Shivantak in the last hours before their world would change forever.

There was someone at the door. "Come," Picard said gravely.

And in a moment, Ambassador Straun was sitting across from Picard in the ready room. His daughter stood beside him. It was astonishing to Picard how their roles had become reversed. For the daughter was afire with the discovery of myriad new worlds to comprehend, but the ambassador was in a daze, his old beliefs gone forever.

The ambassador was still trying to assimilate all the revelations; Picard decided that it was best to leave him in peace.

"The High Shivantak has invited me, and the *Enterprise*'s key crew members, into his august presence," Picard said. "We'll be discussing with him the final disposition of the *thanopstru,* and the details of the rescue mission. But—I see that you will not be coming with us," he added.

"Alas, Captain, I cannot," said Straun.

"But you are his representative to us still, are you not?"

"I cannot reconcile my service to the High Shivantak with the heresy that sits heavy on my heart," said the ambassador softly. "And besides, Captain, I was not invited. And *no one* sets foot uninvited in the High Shivantak's presence—not even an ambassador to an all-powerful alien federation."

"Ambassador Straun, I don't envy your position," said Captain Picard. "I too, once—felt the trauma of being assimilated in an alien culture—my thoughts no longer being my own—everything about who I am dictated by an outside intelligence." The scars of Picard's experience with the Borg would not heal easily, despite the passing of time.

"Captain Picard," said the ambassador, "I would

like to ask you formally what my daughter asked for informally: I do have a sentence of execution hanging over my head, and I think I can genuinely claim that, as it is a sentence for heresy, I am being persecuted for my religious beliefs. My daughter has explained to me how this concept works among your people. I am requesting—asylum."

"And I'm granting it," said the captain. "Good luck to both you and your daughter."

Kio spoke up for the first time, "I didn't say that *I* am asking for asylum, Captain," she said.

"Oh. Forgive me, Kio. I assumed—" Picard thought of the young lieutenant she had been so taken with.

"I'm not going to run away. Oh, I'll travel to the Federation with my father, I'll try to see all I can see—but I'll come back."

"Yes, of course," Picard said.

"Your party is waiting in the transporter room, Captain," the ship's computer said.

"If you'll excuse me," said Picard.

"Of course," the ambassador said, and prepared to be escorted to his quarters.

Chapter Twenty-Two

The Politics
of Self-Destruction

EVERYTHING IN THE AUDIENCE CHAMBER was designed to accentuate the High Shivantak's lordliness and splendor—and to make his supplicants appear as puny and humble as possible. Lord Kaltenbis, the chamberlain, stood at the foot of the throne, and though Picard was the representative of the Federation itself with its myriad worlds, he was not permitted to address the High Shivantak directly, but only through this intermediary.

From Picard's vantage point, the High Shivantak seemed little more that a blur of gold and brightly colored feathers. As Kaltenbis spoke, the blur moved; the captain could see arms waving. Then, it seemed, Kaltenbis began backing down the throne in a hurry. By the time he reached the floor level, he seemed quite out of sorts. In fact, he glared at Picard, and left the chamber without a word.

The High Shivantak rose.

These people certainly had a sense of the majestic. As soon as he was on his feet, trumpets blasted from seven corners of the chamber. Courtiers, round about the hall, fell on their faces, not daring to gaze on the High Shivantak's face.

The Shivantak clapped his hands.

Soundlessly, the audience chamber emptied. It was like magic. The stream of people were simply siphoned off into corridors and hallways, in a ritual that had clearly been practiced a thousand times.

The man who came down the steps was robed in the accoutrements of godhood, but there was no godliness in his face. Instead, Picard observed some very human emotions: concern, instability, and insecurity.

"I have done what no High Shivantak has ever done," he said gravely. "Never in five thousand years of recorded history. I have dismissed everyone from the high chamber. Therefore there will be no record of what we speak, no remembrance, no recollection. This moment is outside history; if we will it so, it will not have happened. Do you understand what I'm saying, Captain Picard?"

"Yes, Your Radiance," said the captain. "On Earth, where I come from, this was known as deniability."

"Ah, politics," said the High Shivantak. "Our cultures may have a wealth of differences, but always there are the people plotting behind the scenes; always there are secret meetings; I've been reading up a little on your history, Captain."

"The Federation isn't perfect," Picard said, smiling a little. "We haven't always done the right thing, but we've evolved some basic principles that we believe in—and that we try to live by."

"Indeed. But here, in this quadrant of what we have just discovered to be a very populated galaxy indeed, the Federation, imperfect as you call it, seems to be the larger reality; and it is always the destiny of the larger reality to dictate to the smaller; truth is defined, I think, as the confluence of many private illusions, and the majority must prevail; how strange it is for me, who have always been at the center of my own pocket universe, to discover that I am a minority, and my whole worldview an illusion spun from ignorance! You see, Captain, how it is with me."

"Birth is always painful, rebirth yet more so," said Picard, quoting the Thanetian holy book.

"I see that you know the Panvivlion," said the High Shivantak, smiling also, though Picard could see the strain behind that smile. "Or is it simply that your handlers have distilled for you that which would be most pleasing to my ear?"

"You give me too much credit, Your Radiance," said Picard. "I'm not a trained diplomat, merely a starship captain."

"Then allow us to be honest with you, Captain."

They were eye to eye now, and Picard sensed that the High Shivantak had rarely allowed himself to appear this vulnerable. And yet, he knew, even vulnerability could be a political tool, and even the end of the world could be the endgame of a cosmic chess match. "For years—ever since my elevation to the Shivantakate—I've believed there might be more to the universe than what is described in the great book. But such beliefs, of course, being heresy, and I, of course, being the guardian of all orthodoxy, have never given utterance to such beliefs. We have been waiting for millennia for the end of the world, Captain, and the end of the world seemed clearly to be coming, right on schedule; and that is my problem. That is the reason I've had two reactions to each of the astonishing events that have plagued this last year of my rule—the public and the private. Publicly, I condemned Straun sar-Bensu to execution for heresy; privately, I sent him to the *Enterprise* to continue to engage in a dialogue with the very aliens who spawned that heresy.

"Now you have come to me, and you have sent me the data record synthesized for me by your Commander Data; and I have experienced the simulation of the events of five thousand years ago with mixed emotions. You understand how it must be for me: to see a sister culture so like ourselves, so committed to our destruction, and to know that we too were once motivated by such mindless hate, even though in this incarnation of Thanet's civilization the past survives only as garbled mythology."

"I realize that it's been trying for you—"

"More than trying. And that is why, even now, we must have a public as well as a private solution. If the end of the world is to be averted, it must happen in a way that does not jar with our worldview—or else—or else, Captain Picard, there will be chaos!" There was silence in the chamber, the kind of silence that follows a statement of unpleasant but irrefutable truth. Despite his wealth and power, the High Shivantak's position was not enviable. The preservation of his subjects' lives counted for little if those lives were stripped of all meaning.

"My underlings here—they think they protect me completely from the outside world," the High Shivantak continued. "The many gifts your people have given us—they locked them away in a secret treasure chamber, hoping, perhaps, that no one would ever look upon them. But in the small hours of the night, when none of my attendants dared disturb me—ah, then, Captain Picard, I wandered through the corridors of this palace, through secret passageways even the servants do not know about, and I saturated myself in the Federation's myriad cultures! I've watched a Klingon ten-opera cycle from beginning to end. I've listened to the cold logic of Vulcan poetry. Yet as much as I've learned from your cultures, I have still found nothing that will help me save the souls as well as the lives of my people."

The saving of souls as well as lives. Many people had grappled with like dilemmas in the course of human history. So many times the end of the world had been predicted, and so many times the Apocalypse had failed to arrive.

The Apocalypse. Wasn't there an ancient book by that name? It dated back to ancient Rome, and presented a similar scenario.

Then, slowly, Captain Jean-Luc Picard began to smile.

"Your Radiance," he said, "I have a suggestion."

Chapter Twenty-Three

The Life of One Child

FIVE THOUSAND YEARS of rage. Would a few hours of compassion temper it? Was there still a recognizably humanoid intelligence in that mass of flesh and metal, or was this cyborg more machine than person?

He floated in the tank. Now and then there came another tear from the corner of an ever-open eye. Aside from that, not a glimmer of emotion.

The life signs were powerfully present. But what would happen if the boy were removed from the comet? Her preliminary findings had been that it could not be done.

She tried again and again, shifting parameters, altering probabilities. But it was clear to Beverly Crusher that boy and machine were so thoroughly integrated that they could not be separated. This was not a matter of a few Borg-like appliances slapped onto a human body that still walked and talked like an independent being. Though the boy's body, preserved in the nutrient tank, looked human, his entire nervous system had been replicated in silicon and extended over the entire *thanopstru*. The frontal lobe of his brain had been invaded by artificial neurons, and fibrous masses of them prevented the extraction of the original brain. Only the most primitive area of the brain remained completely organic and intact—it was that area that was the seat of all that rage, that area that had caused tears to flow from ancient tear ducts despite the conscious mind's lack of awareness of the eyes and other external organs.

The more data came in from her medical tricorder, the less sanguine Beverly Crusher was. She didn't want to lose hope. After all, this boy was the last survivor of an ancient civilization. And he was just a kid.

"How's your research going?" Deanna Troi had beamed into the corridor, and was squeezing her way into the tiny control chamber. "The captain says there's not much time left."

"Do you feel anything?" Beverly said.

"Only the rage," Deanna said. "And underneath the rage, there's a sense of—fulfilment. He knows his mission has reached the final stage."

"We're going about this all wrong," Beverly said. "We're being too humancentric. I've been thinking, if we can only pull the boy's body loose from the matrix of artificial neurons, we'll have a kid to save—but that's wrong, isn't it? The boy's body is an empty shell. His *real* body is the comet."

Deanna closed her eyes. Beverly could see her stiffen as empathic vibrations racked her mind.

"What do you feel?" Beverly said.

"Loneliness. Rage."

Deanna was trembling.

"Let's get back to the *Enterprise*," said Beverly.

The conference room was packed and tense. Deanna, sitting at the opposite end of the table from the captain, was barraged with contradictory emotions. If only they had felt what she felt—*truly* felt it!

"Captain," Worf was insisting, "we have no right to make the *thanopstru*'s decisions for it. Even though it is a child, it has chosen a glorious death in warfare, and it would be dishonorable to deny it that."

"Is there a way we can buy time?" Picard said. "Mr. La Forge."

"Primitive technology, but we could weld some thrusters onto the planet-facing side of the comet and force it off course—send it veering off into space, perhaps slingshotting it against Thanet's gravity well," La Forge said. "The comet would have to cooperate, though."

"How can we guarantee the *thanopstru*'s cooperation?" Picard looked at the others.

"We need to calm his rage," Deanna said. "The anger is what drives that comet. Perhaps if he could start communicating with other people—children his own age, even."

"Work on it," Picard said. "How long until you can get your thrusters in place, Mr. La Forge?"

"The ship's computer has some ancient blueprints; a couple of replicators should be able to spit them right out. We'll just need a couple of people to beam onto the comet's surface and mount them. A pinpoint phaser blast could ignite them—I would say a half hour. And we should know within the hour if it's going to work—plenty of time left to destroy the comet if not."

"Make it so," Picard said.

"Captain," said Worf. "Should we bring back all the Federation personnel to the ship? As a security measure—in case we fail."

"Who is left?"

La Forge said, "Dr. Halliday and his son—and Commander Data. Dr. Halliday specifically asked to remain as long as possible; he thinks that the end-of-the-world festivities are of anthropological interest. And Lieutenant Tarses, sir. He's down there at the request of Kio sar-Bensu."

"Make sure they know that we will beam all of them up from the planet's surface in sixty minutes. If all goes well, they can always return."

"I'll tell them," said La Forge.

Thanet floated serenely beneath them, but the activity on the comet's surface was far from serene.

Worf and two crew members, Patricia Ballard and Joe Byers, had beamed onto the comet's surface. The young Norwegian ensign, Engvig, had come along too, and was quietly observing in the background, doubtless gathering material for his next prize-winning essay. The thrusters Geordi La Forge had rigged up were light, made from a titanium alloy; each contained a powerful miniature energy coil capable of short, sharp bursts of enough energy to slingshot the comet away from its trajectory and out into deep space.

The Klingon was on his guard as always; the crew members, lumbering in their pressure suits and magnetic shoes, seemed to be treating it as a routine job, just like any other starship repair.

"Be wary," Worf barked into his communicator. "This is to be treated with the same precautions as boarding an enemy vessel."

Inside the comet, more activity: Deanna Troi was communicating with Artas once more. A small viewscreen had been beamed aboard the comet with her; it connected directly to the *Enterprise*'s onboard school. Images of happy children: it was their snack break time, and they were laughing, running around in a holographic meadow. Deanna knew that Artas could sense things that happened in the chamber; there were eyes and ears in the inner room, sensors in the walls, designed to safeguard against intrusion and sabotage no doubt. On the little screen, four children were in music class now, struggling through a Mozart string quartet. It was a little painful to hear, but the delight in their faces was infectious. She wondered if Artas could feel it.

I'm back, she called out in her mind. *I've brought you friends.*

The children on the viewscreen stopped playing, waved. "Artas!" they called out.

I don't have friends. I only have the hate.

"Look, Artas—how long has it been since you've played with other children?" She spoke aloud now, so that the children on the *Enterprise* could listen in.

I am not here to play. I'm here to hate.

"Do you want to know their names?"

The children of the *Enterprise* came up to the screen, one by one. There was slender Rosita and chubby Kudaka. "Hello, Artas," they said. Not all of them were sweet: one was quite grumpy, another rubbed his eyes and wanted to go back to his nap.

Who are these children? came Artas's voice.

"They're here to say hello to you—because you've been without friends for so long. They want you to join them."

Join them! This is temptation. I was warned there would be temptations.

"No, Artashka."

How did you know my baby name?

"I heard your mother call you by it—five thousand years ago."

You are my mother—I asked you that when you

229

first came here. And you wouldn't tell me. Only my mother ever called me that. Why aren't you telling me the truth?

"I *am* telling you the truth, Artas. I saw your mother in—a vision—and she saw me. She thought I was an angel, but I'm really an—alien."

Alien?

"Yes. From a planet that's neither Tanith or Thanet."

There are no worlds besides Tanith and Thanet— two peoples locked in an endless conflict—the positive and the negative—death and birth—love and hate—the dance of the two worlds keeps the cosmos in motion.

"That's in your Holy Book, but the people who wrote it didn't know about the other worlds—listen—"

Kudaka, on screen, smiled shyly and said, "I'm from Earth, but Deanna's part Betazoid, that's why you and she can talk better than we can."

T'Paruv, a solemn boy, said, "My parents are from Vulcan. It is illogical for you to be doing what you are doing. The war has been over for five thousand years, and Tanith is no more."

This is a trick!

"No, it's not. I promised your mother—in my vision—that I would save you—that I would not let you perish in vain," Deanna said.

It isn't in vain! What you're showing me now is worse than if you'd just let me do what I have to do. My mother's death needs to be avenged. And my brother Indhuon. And even the Shivan-Jalar, who raised my mother up to glory in the moments before our world was destroyed. Why are you trying to tell me to change?

"Because the universe has changed, Artashka," Deanna said softly. "The cosmos is no longer what you were taught. And you, Artashka, are no longer what you were taught to believe yourself to be."

I am the thanopstru. *I am the god.*

The children were playing leapfrog in the holographic garden—there was a rainbow in the sky— soft music, childish laughter—

Do not tempt me.

A voice in Deanna Troi's ear: "Progress report, Counselor?"

"I'm having a dialogue, of sorts, Captain," she responded. "Little else."

"The thrusters are just about in place, Captain," came the voice of Worf, from the comet's surface.

I heard that! came Artas's voice. *You tricked me! I'm going to destroy all of you.*

As the last thruster was bolted into position, it all began to unravel. Worf was just reporting back to the *Enterprise* when the surface of the comet began to buckle around them. Metal plates ground against each other. Cracks formed in the crust now, and through the cracks a cold blue lightning flashed.

A metal tendril pushed out through a crack. It was jointed, segmented, like an earthworm. It writhed, wrapped itself around one of the thrusters, and yanked—

Worf whipped out a phaser, launched a bolt of lethal lightning at the tentacle. Like a living thing, it thrashed about—evaporated abruptly in a shower of sparks and metal dust—

More tendrils now, twisting, thrusting, retracting. Suddenly, Worf noticed a tendril uncoiling its way toward Ballard.

"The lieutenant!" he shouted.

Suddenly, Ensign Engvig was there, darting toward Ballard, trying to fend off the metal snakes.

"Do not be a hero, Ensign!" Worf shouted. "Let us handle this!"

One seized Lieutenant Ballard and began to squeeze and—

"Commander, it's gonna puncture my pressure suit and—" Worf heard the young lieutenant's voice in his ear.

The tendril caught Engvig, too! It wound its way around him and Ballard, tightening, jabbing. Worf could see the young man's eyes.

Worf and Byers fired repeatedly. The comet's surface quaked again, ruining their aim. Lines of concentrated light lanced the blackness, dissipated in empty space. Ballard was writhing in the grip of the tendrils and—

The metal tentacles came thick and fast now, pushing their way up from the surface, surrounding the lieutenant, throttling, squeezing harder and—

Ballard's scream was cut off and—

Worf winced. It was too late to help her. And

Engvig's suit would be breached in seconds unless—

Ballard exploded in the unforgiving vacuum.
Bloodred mist hung around the limp pressure suit, il-
lumined by Thanet's reflected light. Pieces of the
suit were drifting toward Thanet.

The explosion had been eerie and silent in the air-
lessness of space. Now, as they watched helplessly,
the tentacles were ripping out the thrusters, and one
of them was making its way toward Byers.

"Enterprise, Enterprise," Worf shouted, "get a
lock on us and get us *out* of here!"

*You tricked me! But I'm not turning away from
vengeance.*

"No! I need another chance!" Deanna was saying as the familiar dislocation of the transporter
tingled about her and she vanished from the inner
chamber—

They danced in the streets, clung together with a
feverish desperation, and Simon told Kio stories
about the Romulans—and Earth. On Thanet, the
continents were clustered at the equator—there was
no cold country, no land of the midnight sun.

"I can't help it—deep down, I *still* believe this is our
last hour together—that the world will end," Kio said.

They kissed.

And kissed again.

* * *

Data followed Adam down to the wharf. The boy was stuffing himself with end-of-the-world cakes, talking up a storm. "I'm not going back to the institute when we leave Thanet, Data. It would be like going back to jail. I mean, I've had a whole planet to wander about in. And look at all the stuff I've seen— they can't keep me in a place like that even if I *am* a genius."

Data paused to take in the scene at the wharf. There were hundreds of boats, all lit up, longboats with elaborately carved sterns and prows, and out in the bay, a *dailong* breasting the tide with a hundred *dailong* riders waving torches, and bonfires burning everywhere.

By the water, celebrants were banging drums, leaping, laughing. A group of naked dancers ran up and down the steps, slashing at each other with scythe-shaped knives. From time to time, one collapsed, bleeding, while the others ignored him.

"Oh, it's the death dancers," Adam explained. "They've been practicing this dance since childhood, but until tonight they only used wooden knives. Tonight's the real thing, it's like the culmination of everything they worked for and was passed down to them from generation to generation."

They walked on. "And over there," Adam said, pointing, "those are the prophets. Look at them." They stood on boxes, on makeshift flat boulders, and each one of them was shaggy-haired and bearded and wore nothing but a tattered loincloth or an ill-fitting robe, and each was calling upon his audience to repent, to make sure they were reborn in the new world pure and unstained by sin.

Musicians banged on makeshift instruments. In one corner a bard sang while his lyre emitted patterns of striated light. In a small square surrounded by stalls that sold images of the gods, children forlornly skipped rope.

"You can tell by the caste-mark on their foreheads," Adam told Data, "these kids would have been going through a *Mahal Fartash* ceremony next year, where they'd be chosen by one of the elite training schools—kinda like the institute I got put into, except that they were really looking forward to it, I guess."

The boy was an inexhaustible source of facts. Data filed away each tidbit; all the data on Thanet would be assembled, all the images preserved; the Federation thrived on information.

"You have observed a great deal," Data said.

"Human children," Adam said, "can observe a lot—and nobody observes them. They don't realize that we're watching."

"That is like me," Data said. "I gather background information constantly; I cannot help myself; it is my basic operational mode. But because I resemble humans, they sometimes forget how much I have absorbed."

"I knew we'd get along," Adam said.

"Are we getting along?"

"Sure," Adam said, laughing.

"You're the best friend I ever had," he said suddenly.

"Why?"

"Because you can always make me laugh, and because you're really patient with me. No one else is. It's always, 'Adam, not now,' or 'Adam, shut up.' "

"I am honored to receive your friendship, and I shall try to prove worthy of it," said Data. "Was that a good response?"

"The best," Adam said.

They had wandered far from the pier now, through alleys and into a labyrinthine marketplace which amazingly enough was doing brisk business—though Data noticed that little money was changing hands. Instead, the sellers in their canvas-covered stalls were giving everything away.

"A beautiful rug, sir," said an old woman, gripping his arm. "My family spent a year weaving it— let it be yours for the last minutes of this cycle, so that my family can claim the karmic virtue of generosity and be reborn in a higher caste—"

Data looked at the soft tapestry, realizing it must have taken intense labor, all of it by hand. "I could not deprive you of such a treasure," he said.

"Take it," said Adam. "It's *pau-shafar,* a sacred gift; refusing is very bad manners on this planet."

"But Adam," Data said, "I know it is a very valuable object, and I also know that the world is not *really* going to end in half an hour! So it would feel as though I am cheating her."

"Still, take it," Adam said.

It was silky smooth. It was so sheer that it folded easily into a square that he could throw over one shoulder, yet it felt strong. The images it depicted were wondrous scenes of ancient Thanetian mythology: the emergence of the first *dailong* from the primordial ocean, the divine cycle of the cosmos, the sacred mandala of the High Shivantak. The pictures moved, for the fibers of which the rug was woven were programmed with a short-term color memory algorithm—though the look was primitive, the technology assuredly was not.

The narrow aisles of the market, which operated under an awning of translucent canvaslike material through which one could still see the constant displays of fireworks in the sky above, were crammed with people, all trying to give things away. As quickly as the merchants handed away their treasures, the recipients tried to unhand them. Members of the beggar caste, traditionally near the bottom of the hierarchy, were decked in finery, with *quashgai* feathers and pointed pagoda hats that would have cost a lifetime's panhandling.

"Take my seven-jeweled ring, my alien friend," said one merchant to Data, pressing it into his hand.

"Take it, take it," Adam said, stuffing another valuable bauble into his pocket. "If you feel guilty, you can always give it back when the world doesn't end."

Data paused to listen to a communication from the ship.

It was Worf's gruff voice. "All Federation citizens still on Thanet will be transported back to the ship in six minutes," he said. "The mission to save the child Artas has failed, I repeat, failed; the comet will be destroyed as soon as everyone is safely on board the *Enterprise*."

"Adam, we must go."

Chapter Twenty-Four

The Comet's Song

THE TRANSPORTER ROOM was in chaos. Deanna was materializing from within the comet, Worf and a shaken Byers from the surface, while Engvig was being transported directly to sickbay, and various Federation stragglers from the planet—Dr. Halliday, Kio, and Simon Tarses—were coming through now.

Geordi La Forge was there to greet them and to order all the relevant personnel to the bridge to witness the destruction of the comet.

The transporter thrummed again. This time it was Data and Adam.

"Adam!" said Halliday. "You shouldn't go wandering like that—"

"You never stopped me before," Adam said. "Besides, Data and I made a discovery that—"

La Forge interrupted them. "We only have a few moments. Captain Picard is about to give the order."

"Ballard is dead," said Worf. "She died with honor. I believe that some of her remains may yet be recovered."

On the bridge, the mood was solemn. On screen, the *thanopstru* was about to intersect the upper atmosphere of Thanet; in fifteen minutes, it would do so, and the friction of the air would cause its outer layers to glow like a second sun; it would be too late at that point to annihilate the comet, because the planet-destroying weapons within it would be triggered too close to the surface.

Deanna Troi stood between the captain and Commander Riker. Picard realized that she was more deeply conflicted than any of the others. For them, this was still a simple matter of saving an entire world; but she had seen into the heart of the weapon's mother, had made promises to her—

"Counselor Troi," Picard said mildly, "you may be excused if you like."

"Thank you, sir. But I feel the least I can do is stay," Troi said.

He patted her arm with a strong sympathetic hand.

Ambassador Straun had shed his diplomatic robes and was now wearing a simple off-duty jumpsuit; he looked well, Picard thought. His robes had dwarfed him; now he seemed more in command of his fate.

Kio sar-Bensu came rushing in, followed by

Simon Tarses. She ran to her father and embraced him. "Father, Father—I'm proud of you," she said. She seemed radiant.

"Are you ready, Mr. La Forge?" he asked.

"Whenever you are, Captain!" came the voice of La Forge from down in engineering.

"In that case, you may commence the countdown upon my—"

At that moment, a very agitated Adam Halliday entered, followed by Commander Data.

"Captain, you gotta listen," Adam said. "Data has an idea—an intuitive leap, actually. You should be proud."

Data began to sing.

From his lips there came not the soft-spoken, overly grammatical utterance of an android, but something eerily different. It was the voice of an ancient woman, inconsolable at the loss of a child, and the song was the haunting melody of Taruna's lullaby.

The melody began simply, but on the phrases *copper ring, silver chain, crown of gold* the music arced upward in an elaborate melisma. The voice cracked on the high notes; the very crevices of the song seemed filled with an ancient dust. This was the voice of Taruna, Artas's mother—if she had lived another five thousand years, if every one of those years had been filled with longing for her lost child. Data had somehow imbued this unsophisticated folk tune with a timeless pathos.

Even Worf seemed visibly moved. Was he thinking of the parallels to some Klingon opera? Picard knew immediately what Data's plan must be. And he concurred with it.

"Open a channel to the *thanopstru*," he said. "I think we need Artas to hear this song."

"Yes, sir," said Geordi La Forge.

On screen they saw the heart of the comet now, the boy in his tank, a close-up of his emotionless face and ever-open eyes.

"Begin the countdown," Captain Picard said. "I am not holding up the mission—but you may proceed simultaneously with the lullaby."

"Aye, sir!" came the voices of Data and La Forge simultaneously.

"Four minutes," the computer said. "Three minutes, fifty seconds."

"Counselor Troi," Picard said. "What do you sense?"

Still that rage. The rage was like a roiling, twisting, red-hot cloud, billowing about, with the boy's cold determination as its still small center.

Deanna reached out. She tried not to flinch from all that anger. She could feel the boy resist the probing of her mind—after all, he had similar talents to her, that was one reason he had been selected for this task. She could feel him erect emotional brick walls to keep her out. And yet the walls were crumbling even as he shored them up.

Deanna said, "He senses a new trick, a new way to undermine him. He's even angrier."

How could so much rage emanate from one mind? There had to be a breaking point—there had to be.

"He hears the music," she said.

And the lullaby filled the air, on the bridge as well as in the heart of the comet. Toward the end the song soared up, strained for a high note that never came; and then the melody plummeted once more, ending in a lugubrious half-sigh.

"Your mother sang this to you," Straun was telling his daughter, "when she rocked you in her arms—I haven't thought of her in so long—I thought it was some quaint peasant song from her home island—I didn't know—"

"I remember," Kio said, and she was weeping.

"Twenty seconds," the computer said. "Fifteen. Ten, nine, eight."

Worf said, "Captain, there is a change in the *thanopstru's* vector."

Abruptly, on screen, the boy's eyes closed.

"I feel sorrow," Deanna said. "Loss."

Truly, after five thousand years, the boy was allowing himself to feel grief for the first time. After the mindless and insensate rage—the mourning. And finally—

Tears streamed down the boy's cheeks, melded with the thick nutrient fluid.

"I feel resignation—I feel—deeply hidden beneath the suffering—a kind of joy."

How had this nugget of joy, of goodness, survived all that terrible programming? *Truly,* Deanna thought, *there is a core of goodness within the spirit of all sentient beings—no matter how much we may try to bury it in evil.*

"Captain," came La Forge's voice, "there is a tremendous surge of energy coming from the comet—I think it's . . . reversing course by itself."

"On screen," said Picard.

The boy's face faded. Now they could see Thanet floating against the starstream; Klastravo, its sun, burned far beyond. In the foreground, the comet was coming to a shuddering halt, moments short of hitting Thanet's ionosphere.

"Captain," Deanna said, "the rage is stilled. I'm feeling—sleep. The sleep of a child in its mother's arms."

"Stand down from destruct mode," ordered Commander Riker as Picard nodded his assent.

The comet was changing direction. It was using the planet's gravity as a slingshot, sending itself back out into deep space, away from Klastravo, away from death.

"Will he—die, Counselor?" Ambassador Straun asked.

Deanna closed her eyes. Although Artas was receding from her range, his emotions were so powerful, so amplified by five thousand years of solitude that they still infiltrated her psyche.

"I'm getting a stream of images—a field of billowing grass. An ocean. A wind. A boy running through the open meadow. The embrace of a woman.

It's Artas. He's sleeping," she said. "He's dreaming sweet dreams."

As the *thanopstru* made its way toward the darkness, it appeared less and less like a weapon of death, and more and more like that eternal symbol of hope and of wishes come true—the shooting star.

"Permission to return planetside, Captain?" Simon Tarses asked.

"Unfinished business, Lieutenant?" Picard said.

"Aye, sir."

"Now hear this," Picard announced. "We are not meddlers—at least, never by choice. All unfinished business on Thanet is to be concluded by 0700 hours, at which point we will steal away and leave the people of this world to their own rebirth."

There was a silence; then slowly, one by one, the crew members began to applaud, until, as the sleeping death star disappeared into blackness, the applause surged over Deanna's senses like a tide, buoying her up, calming her fractured spirit.

Chapter Twenty-Five

The Bells of Shivan-Saré

MOMENTS BEFORE THE END of the world, Simon Tarses and Kio sar-Bensu beamed into the grand forum in front of the High Shivantak's citadel. It was as though they had not left. Everywhere were the celebrants, leaping, chanting, banging on timbrels and cymbals. The sky was alive with fireworks exploding into shapes of exotic flowers and insects. From hot-air balloons above the square, orchestras of children blowing on giant seashells played enthusiastic, strident antiphonies. From the highest parapet, a lit window could be seen. As Kio and Simon squeezed their way through the tumult, they could hear people muttering that the High Shivantak would soon show himself—that the great Bells of Shivan-Saré would finally sound.

"The bells?" Simon asked a man who was passing out *zul* cakes.

"They were built at the dawn of time," said the old man, "and they will sound only in the moments before the destruction of the world."

"Where are they?"

"Somewhere in the bowels of the High Shivantak's palace," he said. "You're an alien, aren't you?"

"Yes."

"And yet you remain here with us. I see that it's love that keeps you here, that makes you willing to brave the fiery baptism and rebirth."

Simon blushed and looked at Kio, who was smiling shyly.

They kissed. And Simon remembered another kiss, another time.

"I was thinking about that too," Kio said.

"You're a telepath?"

"No. But sometimes—" The fireworks were coming thick and fast now, the sky was brilliant with patterns of gold, great gashes of neon blue and vermilion. "Sometimes we just think alike. I know you were thinking something like—five thousand years ago, maybe that *was* us, maybe we were those people in another life. Their lives fit us so readily, like clothes we've worn so many times that they drape to our bodies just so."

"But—my culture doesn't believe in reincarnation." And Reincarnation. He hadn't given it much thought before he met Kio, but now— It seemed like a fine idea, the soul going on and on, from time to time, even from world to world.

"Stop! Listen."

There came an ominous rumble, so deep-toned that it seemed to shake the very foundations of the plaza.

The crowd broke out into an uproar. *The Bells of Shivan-Saré!* It was time! The cycle was ending! As if at a signal, with astonishing precision and solemnity, the crowd fell prostrate, facing the topmost parapet of the High Shivantak's palace.

"Look at them!" Worf said. "Utterly fatalistic."

A wall of Ten-Forward, which normally showed a view of space around the *Enterprise,* was now transmitting images of the Shivantak's citadel.

"As the view pans across the crowd," Data said, scanning the viewscreen in far greater resolution than a human eye could, "I do note that two out of the thousands are *not* prostrate."

"And who might they be?"

"Lieutenant Simon Tarses, and Kio, daughter of the Thanetian ambassador," said Data.

Like a death knell, the Bells of Shivan-Saré boomed over the throng. The Thanetians lay with their faces flat against the ground, in a position they had learned in childhood.

The bell tolled. Data knew that its sound would be picked up and broadcast over the entire planet. Indeed, the computer was showing more scenes of Thanet now—a lone longship, its crew all prostrate, listening to the knell on a primitive radio; a farm, with the herders lying down next to their *klariot*s, who bleated and gamboled in the windswept grass—and back to the city.

And then it stopped.

The crew were silent, waiting to see what would happen next.

The fireworks ended.

One by one, all the lights in the city were blinking out.

The music was stilled.

Darkness fell on Thanet, a profound, primal darkness such as had been known only at the dawn of their civilization, before artificial illumination, before even the rediscovery of fire; and Data knew that this was the High Shivantak's doing. He could not destroy the world, but he *could* turn off the world's power switch.

The crew held its collective breath.

And in that moment of ultimate darkness, under the alien stars, Simon and Kio, perhaps the only people on the entire planet not bound by its past, embraced with the fervor of the young; they seemed to be saying farewell to childhood as well as to the old Thanet. In the stillness, Simon could almost hear the heartbeat of the world.

Then came another sound.

Simon broke away. In the pale starlight, he could make out shifting shapes. He knew that none of the populace had raised themselves up from the ground; they still awaited death. But something was going on in the palace of the High Shivantak. There were rumblings. Clankings. Sounds like the shifting of giant gears that had not been greased in a thousand years.

What was happening? The very pavement was vibrating now, and then it began to ripple as though the paving stones were shifting, sorting and resorting themselves like the tiles in one of those ancient puzzle games.

Then came the thunder. Not thunder from the sky, but from the many-tiered palace of the High Shivantak. The crack of stone against stone.

"No," Kio was murmuring, "It didn't work—the world is ending anyway!"

He held her tightly.

Then, abruptly, there was light—

Picard entered Ten-Forward in time to hear the first death knell. He watched in fascination as the crowd fell to the ground. He too heard the strange crashing sounds. But from the vantage point of the ship, with its sensitive tracking devices and its ability to compensate for darkness by seeing far into the infrared, Picard and his crew members could see a great deal more than the denizens of Thanet could.

They could see that the seven-tiered citadel was transforming itself. Hydraulic devices were pushing up the sides, changing the lowest levels into towers with mushrooming minaret roofs. The tower that contained the Shivantak's Holy of Holies was slowly descending to the ground. Parapets were folding like the wings of butterflies. The ancient stones sighed as they shifted.

Data said, "The Shivantak's palace was *designed* to reshape itself!"

"How old is that building?" Riker asked.

"The blueprints are encoded in one of the chapters of the Panvivlion," Dr. Halliday said. "I'll be damned—the sacred texts actually had a built-in escape clause, just in case no *thanopstru* showed up to destroy the world."

"But did the High Shivantak *know?*" Worf said.

"Yes and no," Picard said with a mysterious smile.

"How?" the Klingon asked.

"It all boils down to faith, Mr. Worf. Faith in our ability to keep our promise to protect his world—."

"And faith in his planet's ability to protect itself," Dr. Halliday finished.

"Look," said Deanna. "The lights are coming back on in the city."

Simon Tarses and Kio were still the only ones standing when the lights came on; and the people of Thanet were still on their faces, for no one had commanded them to rise.

But the square was not the same square. For one thing, the Holiest of Holiest had disappeared completely. Instead, there was a small house, little more than a cottage, in the center of a plaza; Simon recognized the house, which had once been the gleaming cupola that topped the highest tower in the city, the dwelling place of the god-king.

He held Kio's hand tightly.

Soft music began to play from unseen sources. The door of the house opened, and a man emerged. Simon had to squint to see him; the light that shone around the plaza, pouring from sources concealed within what had once been the palace, was searingly bright; his eyes smarted.

The man wore a simple white robe. He had long, unkempt white hair; he seemed immeasurably old. Simon remembered back on Earth, how some people used to depict God as an old man in a white robe— or sometimes it was Father Time who was depicted that way. This fellow, a little bent with age, was coming down the steps.

When he spoke, the new walls that had risen around them in the darkness reflected his voices, and his words echoed and reechoed; though his was the wheezing voice of an old man, it spoke with authority, and was audible to all.

"Citizens of Thanet," he said, "you have all died and now you are reborn. Look around you; the city is not the city. Search your hearts, and you will know that you are not as you once were. I was once the High Shivantak of this world, but now, as you see, my feet are touching the ground, and therefore I am no longer the most high. And my seat among the clouds has come down to the earth, that the scripture might be fulfilled, which says: 'He that had once been highest became lowest.' You have passed from one life to the next with your memories of the past intact and no sense of passing at all save for a few moments of jarring darkness; this is the miracle spoken of in the Panvivlion, which says: 'You shall be snatched up and returned to a world that is not the world.' Rejoice, Thanetians. And do not weep, that I am no longer your leader. For the Holy Panvivlion decrees that power shall pass to a child, for 'The power to rule passed into the hands of the one child who had shown no fear.' There is in fact such a child among you. For though all of you remain prostrated, hardly daring to gaze upon me, there is one in the crowd who never prostrated herself, who faced the darkness boldly and without any terror of death at all—"

And suddenly Simon knew what must happen next. He turned to Kio. "He's giving you this planet, Kio! A whole world, a whole new people, reborn, for you to lead—"

Kio said, "That's ridiculous," but as she said so, members of the crowd had begun to lift themselves up from the ground, and many began pointing toward her, and then one or two of the less timid approached, began to touch her, the hem of her tunic, even her cheek—and suddenly they had hoisted her up on their shoulders, and they were saying, "Your feet can't touch the ground, you're our new Shivantak now," and they were carrying her toward where the old man was still standing, and someone noticed that Simon had been with her, and he found himself, too, being lifted up, being carried aloft, and the crowd was cheering now, he was riding the sea of Thanetians, like a *dailong* skimming the ocean.

At the center of the plaza, Kio forced them to let her down. She went up to the High Shivantak, who immediately fell to his knees in front of her.

She glanced at Simon, clearly unsure of what she should do next. Simon understood how she felt. He had spent so many years feeling unsure of himself; of where he belonged; and of what he could accomplish. But now, he realized, he was capable of faith after all, if not in himself then in Kio. He smiled at her, willing her to read his thoughts. She smiled back.

"I am yet young," she said, "and if I am to lead the world, I must learn everything I can about the Federation, about the many alien races in our galaxy; for the knowledge we used to have has become meaningless, just as the Panvivlion says. But my first decree is clear: I abolish the caste system. Let each person find his own level in the world, based on his own talents and ambitions."

"There'll be chaos!" someone shouted.

"No," she said. "This is a new beginning. We will begin as equals. And here is my second decree. I am going to leave you. I need to study among the people of the Federation. I need to work out which ideas are best exchanged and which belong exclusively to ourselves. I do not know how long I will be gone for. In the meantime, I appoint as regent the one who was High Shivantak in the previous cycle. I trust he will accept my decision."

Humbly, the Shivantak nodded.

Chapter Twenty-Six

Artas

A MEADOW OF GRAY-GREEN GRASS. A breeze. A deep blue sky. A dark, mysterious sea. Clouds, too, silver clouds fringed with gilt and purple; the moon that danced and the moon that wept.

A bridge across the ocean.

The bridge woven from the insubstantial; from the webs of arachnids in the deep forest, from the shadows of running children, from the fringes of rainbow—and yet the bridge seemed to support his feet as he took a few tentative steps.

Beneath him, the ocean howled. In the distance, a *dailong* breached the tide, and many moons danced over the jeweled waves.

You don't have to forget anymore.

He could hear his mother's voice, singing to him in the wind.

But Mother, why do you sound so ancient?

Time has passed, my son. Time for you to begin to heal.

My anger—

Let it go.

Am I dreaming? Am I truly dreaming?

You have stood at the brink to the country of dreams for five millennia, son, and now you will cross over to the other shore—the far side of the sea.

Are you really my mother?

Yes.

But this is a dream.

You have lived a dream up till this moment.

Am I dead?

Life, death—these are the concerns of those who still inhabit the world of shadows.

Am I to forget?

No, son. Remember. Remember everything. And when you have remembered to the full, as though you downed a full glass of the most potent peftifesht—then let go. Let it all dissipate into the air. And then, when you are ready, cross the bridge. I'll be waiting.

For a long time, Artas stood on the first step. The memories came flooding back. The song was the catalyst. He remembered hearing the song, lying in his mother's warm embrace, long before he even knew the meaning of the words. His mother had heard the song too, and her mother before her; that lullaby was what connected him to pasts beyond remembering, to futures beyond imagining.

He knew he would be ready soon—but he wanted to savor the sound of the ocean—just another moment—just another—another—

Chapter Twenty-Seven

Ready Room

THERE WAS A QUEUE to see the captain; for a few moments, Picard sat back, enjoying rare solitude. But duty called. A captain cannot afford too much of the luxury of aloneness.

The first ones to come in were his officers—one at a time, he commended them, said those things that a captain must say to boost morale and to congratulate them on a job well done. And then there were the arrangements for Patricia Ballard's funeral; Picard had not known her well, but her death saddened him; there had been, perhaps, no need for casualties on this mission.

Perhaps, as the Thanetians believed, her noble sacrifice would allow her to be reborn in a higher caste.

"Next," said Captain Picard. "Ah, Dr. Halliday."

The venerable xenologist barely made it through the door. His son Adam was in tow.

"Good job, Adam," said Picard. "And Dr. Halliday—your reports were invaluable to Starfleet and the Federation. Thank you."

"Just doing my job, Captain," Halliday said, "and gaining a lot of weight in the process. With seventeen castes and hundreds of subcastes and all those dietary laws, there certainly were a lot of dishes to taste on Thanet."

"I have been asked to offer you a temporary consulship on Thanet," said Picard, "until such time as a permanent diplomatic mission is established."

"Yippee!" Adam cried. "We're staying. Can Commander Data stay too?"

"I'm afraid not, Adam. We wouldn't be able to do without him."

"But he was the only one I ever made friends with here."

"I believe Commander Data has a rug he needs to return to someone on Thanet; shall we—lend him to you for a few days?"

"Captain, you're the best!"

"Thank you, Captain," Dr. Halliday added. "I must admit that sometimes I get a little—distracted. But it gives me pleasure when my son is happy."

They said their good-byes.

Then there was the young ensign Envig, his wounds quickly healed through Dr. Crusher's rapid intervention.

"So," Picard said to Tormod, "do you think you'll have something to report back to the prizewinning essay committee?"

"Yes, indeed, sir!" Tormod said.

"Perhaps you'll consider a career in Starfleet in the future; I am sure I can provide a letter of recommendation. As long as you keep those grades up."

"Yes, sir," said Tormod, saluting smartly. "In these past days, I've done *everything*—I've helped rescue a planet, lived through a diplomatic crisis, seen a millennia-long feud averted, and made friends with some great people. I've touched history, Captain, shaken its hand. If this is what a week in Starfleet is like, I can imagine what an entire career would be—"

The next person to come in was Lieutenant Simon Tarses. He was with Kio sar-Bensu—and she looked particularly fetching in uniform, for Picard had made her an acting ensign for the duration of the voyage back to Earth.

"Lieutenant Tarses reporting, sir."

"A mission well done, Lieutenant," the captain said.

"May I say—may I—"

"Permission to speak freely granted, crewman."

"Sir, since that incident when you—defended me—all those years ago—I've been torn. Those accusations made me feel like a perpetual alien, neither human nor Romulan, someone no one dared trust. The things you said were the right things, sir, but they didn't totally hit home until—"

"Until you met a certain person?" Picard said, smiling.

"Yes, sir," Tarses said. "I met someone equally torn between two worlds."

Kio sar-Bensu, lately named ruler of an entire planet, who had set her power aside in order to fulfill her quest for knowledge, only smiled.

"Well, what about you, Kio sar-Bensu?" the captain asked, smiling.

"I'm thinking of going to school on Earth for a while, Captain. Starfleet Academy, if they'll have me."

Tarses looked wistful. Undoubtedly he was calculating how long it would be before *Enterprise* returned to this sector. Quite some time, alas. Picard glanced down at the blank padd on his desk.

"Mr. Tarses, this duty roster says you're due for some shore leave." The young crewman looked confused.

"But, sir, I just had a week on—" Kio nudged him.

"Oh. Oh! Thanks—I mean, thank you, sir!"

After the two left, there seemed to be no one else waiting.

The computer told him the former High Shivantak of Thanet wanted a word with him.

"On screen," Picard said, and he was looking into the face of a man who had changed a world.

"A metaphoric End of Days," the Shivantak marveled. "So simple, yet so brilliant, Captain. Thank you for all you did."

"I did very little, Your Radiance. It was you who executed the plan and spoke so eloquently to your people. It was your wise words that set an entirely new society in motion. But I would like to know something—did you *know* that when you set off the Bells of Shivan-Saré, hydraulic engines would kick in and transform the towers into plazas and the plazas into towers?"

"I had an inkling of it, Captain. But with all such things—you never know what will happen until you push the button."

"I suppose one can never underestimate the power of faith."

"No indeed, Captain Picard. And faith can remain powerful even when we do not take so literal a view of our holy books."

"Ambassador Straun seems to have reached a similar conclusion."

"I regret having had to lie to him and to so many others. My former position required mastery of the greatest magic of all—the art of illusion."

"The world is web of shadows, spun by a master of the dark," said Picard. It was the very opening lines of the Holy Panvivlion. "Are you that master?"

"You are quite the scholar, Captain. Let us just say that—for a brief moment—to quote again from one of your planet's sacred texts—I was the Great and Powerful Oz."

Picard could not help smiling a little. "Adieu," he said softly, as the former god-king's image dissolved into blackness.

Look for STAR TREK fiction from Pocket Books

Star Trek®

Novelizations

Star Trek: Deep Space Nine®

Far Beyond the Stars • Steve Barnes
What You Leave Behind • Diane Carey

#3 • *Cathedral* • Michael A. Martin & Andy Mangels

#4 • *Lesser Evil* • Robert Simpson

Rising Son • S.D. Perry

The Left Hand of Destiny, Books One and *Two* • J.G. Hertzler & Jeffrey Lang

Star Trek: Voyager®

Mosaic • Jeri Taylor

Pathways • Jeri Taylor

Captain Proton: Defender of the Earth • D.W. "Prof" Smith

The Nanotech War • Steve Piziks

Novelizations

Caretaker • L.A. Graf

Flashback • Diane Carey

Day of Honor • Michael Jan Friedman

Equinox • Diane Carey

Endgame • Diane Carey & Christie Golden

#1 • *Caretaker* • L.A. Graf

#2 • *The Escape* • Dean Wesley Smith & Kristine Kathryn Rusch

#3 • *Ragnarok* • Nathan Archer

#4 • *Violations* • Susan Wright

#5 • *Incident at Arbuk* • John Gregory Betancourt

#6 • *The Murdered Sun* • Christie Golden

#7 • *Ghost of a Chance* • Mark A. Garland & Charles G. McGraw

#8 • *Cybersong* • S.N. Lewitt

#9 • *Invasion! #4: The Final Fury* • Dafydd ab Hugh

#10 • *Bless the Beasts* • Karen Haber

#11 • *The Garden* • Melissa Scott

#12 • *Chrysalis* • David Niall Wilson

#13 • *The Black Shore* • Greg Cox

#14 • *Marooned* • Christie Golden

#15 • *Echoes* • Dean Wesley Smith, Kristine Kathryn Rusch & Nina Kiriki Hoffman

#16 • *Seven of Nine* • Christie Golden

#17 • *Death of a Neutron Star* • Eric Kotani

#18 • *Battle Lines* • Dave Galanter & Greg Brodeur

#19-21 • *Dark Matters* • Christie Golden

  #19 • *Cloak and Dagger*

  #20 • *Ghost Dance*

  #21 • *Shadow of Heaven*

Books set after the series

Homecoming • Christie Golden

The Farther Shore • Christie Golden

Enterprise®

Novelizations
Broken Bow • Diane Carey
Shockwave • Paul Ruditis
By the Book • Dean Wesley Smith & Kristine Kathryn Rusch
What Price Honor • Dave Stern
Surak's Soul • J.M. Dillard

Star Trek®: New Frontier

New Frontier #1-4 Collector's Edition • Peter David
  #1 • *House of Cards*
  #2 • *Into the Void*
  #3 • *The Two-Front War*
  #4 • *End Game*
#5 • *Martyr* • Peter David
#6 • *Fire on High* • Peter David
The Captain's Table #5 • *Once Burned* • Peter David
Double Helix #5 • *Double or Nothing* • Peter David
#7 • *The Quiet Place* • Peter David
#8 • *Dark Allies* • Peter David
#9-11 • *Excalibur* • Peter David
  #9 • *Requiem*
  #10 • *Renaissance*
  #11 • *Restoration*
Gateways #6: *Cold Wars* • Peter David
Gateways #7: *What Lay Beyond*: "Death After Life" • Peter David
#12 • *Being Human* • Peter David

Star Trek®: Stargazer

The Valiant • Michael Jan Friedman
Double Helix #6: *The First Virtue* • Michael Jan Friedman and Christie Golden
Gauntlet • Michael Jan Friedman
Progenitor • Michael Jan Friedman

Star Trek®: Starfleet Corps of Engineers (eBooks)

Have Tech, Will Travel (paperback) • various
  #1 • *The Belly of the Beast* • Dean Wesley Smith
  #2 • *Fatal Error* • Keith R.A. DeCandido
  #3 • *Hard Crash* • Christie Golden
  #4 • *Interphase, Book One* • Dayton Ward & Kevin Dilmore

Star Trek® Short Story Anthologies

Strange New Worlds, vol. I, II, III, IV, V, and VI • Dean Wesley Smith, ed.
The Lives of Dax • Marco Palmieri, ed.
Enterprise Logs • Carol Greenburg, ed.
The Amazing Stories • various

Other Star Trek® Fiction

Legends of the Ferengi • Ira Steven Behr & Robert Hewitt Wolfe
Adventures in Time and Space • Mary P. Taylor, ed.
Captain Proton: Defender of the Earth • D.W. "Prof" Smith
New Worlds, New Civilizations • Michael Jan Friedman
The Badlands, Books One and *Two* • Susan Wright
The Klingon Hamlet • Wil'yam Shex'pir
Dark Passions, Books One and *Two* • Susan Wright
The Brave and the Bold, Books One and *Two* • Keith R.A. DeCandido

So, you thought you knew everything there was to know about VOYAGER®....

For seven years, Captain Kathryn Janeway and the crew of the aptly named Starship Voyager™ lived with one goal—to get home—and strove to live up to the ideals of Starfleet as they traveled alone in a   tumultuous region of space. Relive their epic journey through summaries, photos, and detailed episode data in this official companion to Star Trek: Voyager, the series that proved once again the power of Star Trek.

STAR TREK
VOYAGER®
COMPANION

COMING SOON!

VGRC.01

STAR TREK

STCR